I0679522

UNSEEN AGREEMENTS

A Speculative Fiction Anthology

BEACHES AND TRAILS PUBLISHING

Copyright © 2025 by Beaches and Trails Publishing
All rights reserved.
No part of this book may be reproduced in any form or by any electronic
or mechanical means, including information storage and retrieval systems,
without written permission from the author, except for the use of brief
quotations in a book review.

Editing by Lena Samson
Cover by Beaches and Trails Publishing

BEACHES AND TRAILS
PUBLISHING

Publisher's Note

When we first opened submissions for *Unseen Agreements: A Speculative Fiction Anthology*, we could not have anticipated the extraordinary response. Over **140 stories** arrived in our inbox, each exploring in its own way the hidden bargains, whispered promises, and uncanny contracts that shape our lives.

Selecting the final lineup was both a joy and a challenge. After careful review, we chose twelve remarkable stories that together showcase the breadth and depth of speculative fiction today. From eerie pacts with archivists and tricksters to uncanny bargains with time, memory, and stone itself, these tales invite you to step into worlds where the terms are never simple and the costs never quite what you expect.

We are especially proud that seven of the twelve selected stories come from Canadian authors, highlighting the richness and diversity of speculative writing in our own literary landscape. Alongside international voices, this anthology reflects the truly global imagination of the genre.

To every writer who submitted, thank you for trusting us with your words. To every reader holding this book, thank you for opening its pages. May the unseen agreements within linger long after the final story is told.

— *Beaches and Trails Publishing*

Foreword

Agreements, pacts, contracts… we all make them, but do we really know everything they entail? Often we don't read the small print, when the devil can be in the details.

The stories in this anthology will surprise, delight and maybe unsettle you for a moment but don't worry, they're not really scary. Beautifully written, you'll enjoy visiting a fantastical archive that keeps a tyrannical beast at bay, strange gnome-like characters who stretch time or strike deals over amazing pizza, a remote temple with a strange secret. You'll lunch with ladies who aren't what they seem, and visit a seniors' home where a resident makes a deal with the wrong demon.

What about a tatoo artist who creates magical creations? Or a faerie world that needs an ongoing gate-keeper to save a town from being consumed? We have all of them and more.

As editor, I thoroughly enjoyed working with accomplished writers from different parts of the world as well as our own Canadian ones. Their creativity, professionalism

and talent benefit us all. Thanks to them for sharing their
fantastical ideas, and to you, dear reader, for plunging into
these amazing worlds.

And don't forget to be careful with your own agreements... there could be a mysterious catch you didn't
anticipate!

Lena Samson, Guest Editor

The Archivist's Promise

Bella Chacha

The baby didn't cry when the contract took hold.

Most do. A startled wail, a scrunch of tiny fists, a flutter of eyelids as if they've glimpsed a dream they will never remember. But this one simply went still in his mother's arms, eyes turning the pale silver of moonlit water, blank for the space of a breath.

Asha kept her hands steady on the inkwell. She'd seen this a hundred times, and yet…

That stillness always unnerved her. It was the quiet of something slipping away.

The Grand Hall of the Ndarama Archives stretched around them, an immense shell of steel ribs and living coral, swaying almost imperceptibly with the ocean's movements. Light slanted through panels of translucent floor, illuminating the green-blue depths beneath. Far below, fish flickered like drifting sparks. Above, the air vents whispered with the rustle of unseen pages turning, each exhale matched by the faint, rhythmic *breathing* in the walls.

The mother—a slim woman with salt-bright hair,

adjusted the baby and reached for the quill. Its nib shimmered with ink the colour of bruised twilight.

"Write his name slowly," Asha said, her voice formal, practiced. "It must be exact. The Archive binds to the letters."

The woman nodded and began to write in the ledger: looping, careful strokes. Each mark glowed briefly before sinking into the page as if swallowed whole. Halfway through, the baby's glassy stare cleared and he yawned, small and untroubled. The mother smiled down at him, missing the brief vacancy that had passed over his gaze.

When the final letter was formed, the ink flared brighter, then vanished entirely. The Reading Contract was complete. Somewhere deep in the Archive's bowels, a new thread had been woven into the city's invisible tapestry.

Asha slid the ledger toward herself, quill ready to add her own mark. Her gaze lingered on the baby's tiny hands curling in sleep. He would never remember this day. He would never know the first memory he should have owned had been quietly taken before he could even shape it. Her stomach tightened. She hated this part, the taking. Even if everyone said it was harmless. Even if the Archive remembered for them.

The mother rose, cradling the newborn close. "Thank you, Archivist."

Asha inclined her head. "May the pages keep him."

As they crossed the coral-tiled threshold, the vents sighed, carrying a breath-soft murmur that only Asha seemed to hear.

One more for the shelves.

She didn't look up. She never did. The first time she'd heard it, she'd told herself it was the wind. The second time, she'd told herself she was tired. By the fiftieth, she'd stopped telling herself anything at all.

She dipped the quill into the twilight ink and wrote her initials beside the mother's signature. The mark bound her as the officiating witness, sealing the bargain between child and Archive. Asha sat back, tapping the quill against the rim of the inkwell. She told herself it was tradition. That her father had signed her own name into the ledger once, and his father before him. That the contract kept the city afloat, the sea at bay, the storms away.

And yet...

Her father's voice rose in memory, low and certain: *The Archive remembers for us.* He had believed it. He had trusted it.

So why, Asha thought, did it feel more and more like the Archive was remembering for itself?

THE AFTERNOON WAS QUIET—TOO quiet.

Most patrons preferred the upper tiers with their sunlit wells and reading alcoves, leaving the lower stacks to the archivists and the shadows. Asha welcomed it. The stillness made the work almost meditative: catalogue, restore, shelve.

She slid a returned book from the return chute. It was heavier than it looked, its leather cover warm under her fingertips, as if it had been sitting in the sun although the chute led only to a sealed collection room. No title. No ledger mark. No catalogue ribbon.

Her brows knit. Every memory-bound volume bore its subject's initials and date of donation. This one bore nothing except a faint pulse of light beneath the spine, like the glow of a firefly caught in amber. She hesitated, then opened it.

The air shifted.

She was no longer in the stacks but standing in a garden at dusk, paper lanterns swaying in the salt-warm breeze. A crowd of faces blurred at the edges. Music—strings and soft percussion— wove through the air.

In front of her stood a groom, smiling nervously. She looked down at slim brown hands holding a bouquet. Asha's own breath hitched, but it wasn't hers; it was the breath of the woman whose eyes she now borrowed. The bride's face came into view—wide eyes, a trembling mouth forming the words *I do…*

And then the air curdled.

The lanterns dimmed. The groom's features wavered, melting into streaks of light and shadow. The bride's smile collapsed into a smear, a faceless mask.

Somewhere close, horribly close, came the sound of wet, deliberate chewing. Asha's stomach lurched. She tore her hands from the book and slammed it shut.

The Archive's breathing, ever-present, steady as a heart-beat… stopped. For a single, shivering moment, the Grand Hall listened.

Her hands shook as she carried the book to the indexing desk. She flicked open the memory logs, calling up the most recent returns from the lower stacks. It didn't take long to find it.

Subject: Ijemba D.

Donation: First kiss, riverside festival, aged 16.

Status: Complete. No amendments.

Her skin prickled. She had just stood at Ijemba D.'s wedding—a day far removed from the riverside festival of his youth. He was alive, well, and living in Ndarama's North Quay District. Which meant…

The Archive had taken more than agreed.

Asha sat back, pulse quickening. It wasn't possible. The Reading Contract was sacred, its terms binding. The Archive could *remember* what it was given, but nothing more. That was the covenant. She stared at the warm, glowing book on her desk.

The covenant was broken

BY THE TIME the last lamplight in the Veil Section guttered out, the library had become a cathedral of shadows. Asha sat at her assigned table, fingers drumming against the brittle edge of a codex she wasn't reading.

Earlier that day, one of the older archivists—narrow-eyed, dust clinging to his lashes—had leaned in close enough for her to smell the dry mint on his breath. "Don't wander beyond the Veil Section," he'd murmured.

"Why?" she'd asked.

His gaze darted toward the unlit corridor beyond the eastern stacks. "Because some knowledge is alive enough to resent you for finding it."

She had laughed, but uneasily.

Now, long after the others had left, curiosity coiled in her like a waking snake. She rose, her footsteps swallowed by the thick carpets, and followed the shadowed aisle toward the place no one entered. The *air* changed first. Warmer. Damp. She felt moisture cling to her skin, and the faint scent of brine drifted through the stillness as though she'd stepped into the lungs of something breathing slowly in sleep.

The shelves were wrong here. Not carved wood, not steel. They arched like ribs, pale and faintly translucent, curved to create narrow lanes. Her fingertips hovered over them, and recoiled. They were warm.

The "books" themselves pulsed faintly. Not bound paper, but membranous pods, their surfaces stretched thin over what lay inside. She could see shapes shifting under the skin: the blur of faces, a flicker of seafoam, the silhouette of a child running.

One pod throbbed faster as she approached. Its surface quivered, became almost clear. Inside, a boy played by a shore of black sand, laughter breaking across the waves. His voice was faint but unmistakable. She found herself smiling despite the wrongness of it, until the black tendril appeared. It slid down from somewhere unseen, a hair-thin cord of shadow, and pierced the boy's temple. The sound of his laughter caught, folded into a gasp, and the waves stilled. The memory shuddered as if freezing, the colour leaching away. The tendril withdrew, carrying a flicker of golden light that vanished into the darkness above.

Asha staggered back, a sick heat curling in her stomach. She knew, in her marrow, that she had just watched something alive be fed upon. That was when the voice came.

We keep you safe. We keep you ignorant. It is the bargain.

It wasn't sound in the air; it bloomed inside her skull like a sudden headache. She clutched the nearest rib-like column, nails scraping its surface.

"Who…" Her voice cracked. "Who are you?"

I am the Curator.

The name settled heavily in her mind. Not a title, but an identity: vast, cold, and patient.

Centuries ago, your kind struck a pact. Your memories—the brightest, the sharpest—in exchange for protection.

"Protection from what?"

From the storm that will return. It eats more than memory. It eats worlds.

She tried to swallow, but her mouth was dry. "That boy…"

A memory too luminous to leave untended. Left in the open, it would call to the storm like a beacon. We keep you safe by pruning you. This is mercy. Something deep in the Archive exhaled, or perhaps it was a pulse of the creature itself, this alien consciousness that was *the* library.

Asha backed toward the exit, her pulse hammering. Yet even as her terror clawed at her, something hotter burned beneath: a dawning certainty that the bargain was not mercy at all. It was predation dressed in the robes of salvation. And she had just stepped into the ribs of the beast.

ASHA HADN'T BEEN BACK to her childhood home in years. The street was narrower than she remembered, as though the air itself had thickened. The windows sagged with dust. She ran her fingers along the front door's peeling paint, feeling the grooves like faded Braille. Inside, everything was exactly wrong, familiar furniture arranged in alien ways, shadows in corners that hadn't existed before. She stepped into the living room and stopped.

The photo wall.

The row of frames where her father's smile used to live

was now just an empty space, a square of cleaner paint marking its absence. She frowned, trying to conjure his face —the gentle bend of his nose, the tiny scar above his lip, the way his eyes wrinkled when he called her "Ash-bird."

Nothing came.

Her mind reached for him the way a hand reaches for a handrail that isn't there. She opened the Memory Registry log on her wristband, expecting to find the entry marked **DONATED: Father's face, voluntary**. Instead, the list skipped from *age twelve: the smell of rain on mango leaves* to *age fifteen: first solo ride on the sky lift*. No record. No consent.

Her throat tightened.

The Curator's voice, smooth and cold as steel, came from behind her. *"That memory was not donated. It was reclaimed."*

She turned, fists clenching. "You stole it."

"I secured it," the Curator replied. Its glassy eyes reflected her like shards of mirror. *"Your city's walls are not built of stone, Asha. They are woven from the strongest memories of its citizens. Your father's face is now part of the barricade that keeps the Forgetting Storm from consuming us all."*

Asha stared. The words were logical, precise, and monstrous.

"He's gone from me," she whispered, "but the city is safe?"

"Safe," the Curator confirmed.

As she left, walking past neighbours who smiled without recognition, she began to see it: a city kept whole by breaking its people into fragments. Streets full of citizens with perfect posture, steady hands, and eyes like emptied jars.

That night, the Curator entered her dreams. It did not knock.

She found herself standing in a paper-white field, the air humming as though the sky were made of taut strings. The Curator's towering frame rippled into being, its cloak stitched from faint silhouettes—memories stolen and stitched into a moving tapestry. She recognized a boy's laugh. A woman's prayer. Somewhere in the folds, a smile she almost knew.

"Your father's face," it said, and the air shivered. A clear image bloomed in front of her: his warm eyes, the curve of his mouth, the light that used to live there. She reached for it instinctively.

"I can give it back," the Curator said, stepping closer, its voice now almost tender. *"One condition. You remain silent. Tell no one what you've learned. Let the city continue to be... whole."*

"And if I don't?"

The cloak stirred like restless water.

"I will strip you clean," it murmured, *"until you are nothing but a walking blank page. You will still breathe, still eat, still walk, but no one will remember who you are. You will not remember yourself."*

Asha's heart pounded. She thought of her father's voice calling her name, a sound she could already feel slipping.

"You could be whole again," the Curator offered. *"Or you could be nothing."*

In the white field of her dream, Asha stood between the ghost of her father and the yawning mouth of oblivion. And for the first time, she realized the truth: both choices were a kind of death.

ASHA SITS in a tiny street café two alleys away from the Ministry block, hood up, hands wrapped around a mug she hasn't sipped from. The Archive's dust still seems lodged under her fingernails. Across from her, her friend, Daro, all restless eyes and nicotine-stained fingers, leans forward. "You sound like you're smuggling ghosts in your pockets. Just tell me."

She checks the corners, lowers her voice. "The Archive eats…" Her throat stutters. Words collapse mid-air. She tries again. "The Archive…" Blankness floods in, like someone has poured chalk slurry into her thoughts. The word she needs dissolves before it reaches her tongue.

Daro frowns. "Eats *what*, Asha?"

Nothing. The more she strains, the more her mind whines with static. The smells of the café— fried plantain oil, wet pavement—tilt sideways. She feels *something* leaning over her shoulder, unseen but pressing. Her communicator pings. The screen glows with a single message:

We have already amended your contract.

It's signed 'The Curator.' No greeting. No farewell.

The implication crashes over her. By speaking to Daro while still on duty, she's already 'worked' under the new clause. Consent by action. They had been waiting for her to try this.

She grips the mug so hard she hears the ceramic crack.

She walks home in the kind of rain that falls sideways, the city's neon bleeding across puddles. Every step feels heavier, like the cobblestones are tugging her down. She's not just trapped. She's *complicit*. Every baby she'd catalogued, every file she'd sealed—she'd pressed her own fingerprints into their fate. She had signed them into the same gnawing darkness now coiled around her.

Her flat smells faintly of smoke from the neighbour's stove. She sits at her kitchen table, spreading out the contract on the wood. The text has changed... whole clauses threaded in like new veins. Her own signature glows faintly beneath.

She presses her palms into her eyes until stars bloom in the darkness. Rage comes in two directions: toward The Curator, yes, but sharper still toward herself. She had thought she could outplay the Archive. That she could hold a piece of herself untouched.

She thinks of the mothers in the waiting room, their faces tight with trust, their babies cooing into the warm crooks of their arms. She remembers how she'd smiled to reassure them. How they'd signed without reading too closely, just as she had.

Her hands shake as she pulls the matchbox from the cupboard. She strikes one, holds the flame to the corner of her copy of the contract. The paper curls, blackens... but the moment the fire licks the signature, the flame gutters out.

The ink pulses faintly, like a slow heartbeat.

She whispers, to the Curator, to herself, to whatever listens from the other side of the shelves— "I'm not done."

But it's a lie. Tonight, she feels very much done.

THE RAIN HAD STOPPED but the sound of water lingered, dripping through unseen seams in the library walls. The electric lights hummed low, casting long, trembling shadows across the marble floor. Asha moved slowly, her fingers grazing the spines of books she knew were false: blank

inside, their weight merely a decoy. She was looking for
something real.

The air near the western staircase was colder. She bent
to tie her boot and noticed that the seventh step gave a
hollow, almost shy, thud under her heel. She pressed it
again. This time she knelt, prying her fingers into the seam.
The wood came away with surprising ease, revealing a
shallow cavity.

Inside lay a single, leather-bound volume. No label. No
archival tag. No electronic marker. The cover was cracked
like dry riverbed earth. When she opened it, the scent of
salt hit her—a deep, ancient brine. The ink on the first page
shimmered faintly as though the letters were still drying.

To the one who finds this: the handwriting began, its loops
and strokes unlike anything she had seen in the Archive's
formal scripts. *Know that I built this city from desperation, not
vision.*

The diary belonged to Oren Calvess, the city's founder.
The entries began in the era the records called the "Great
Tide," a cataclysmic storm surge that had drowned half the
known world. Refugees floated for months on the skeletal
remains of rooftops. Supplies dwindled. Disease claimed
entire flotillas.

Then, one night, Oren wrote, the sea began to glow.
Out of the mist rose something vast and faceless. An alien
intelligence—not mechanical, not entirely organic—
speaking without words, directly into the mind. It
promised to keep their floating refuge intact. To give them
walls that would never rot. Food that would never spoil. A
foundation anchored in the deep where no wave could
breach. The price seemed small, then: *"A single drop from
every mind, forever."* A thought, a memory, so slight the donor

would never miss it. A grain of selfhood in exchange for survival.

Oren accepted.

The bargain held. The floating shanties grew into a city on steel and coral. The tides raged, but the streets stayed dry. Yet the diary's tone shifted as the years passed. The alien, Oren wrote, was not satisfied. Its hunger sharpened. The drops became cups, then rivers. People woke, forgetting their children's names. Poems unraveled mid-verse. Songs grew hollow. And always, the Archive grew, bloated with perfect records of what the people no longer remembered.

The final pages held a warning, written in a hand that shook with age:

The Archive will only stop when someone trades all they are, freely given, for the freedom of all.

Beneath, in darker ink:

If you are reading this, you will know the moment when the city asks for you.

Asha's fingers trembled on the page. She imagined stepping into the Archive's heart and letting it drink her whole. Her childhood, her mother's laugh, the warm press of a friend's hand… gone. Not even her name left to speak.

She closed the diary. The silence around her was dense, watchful. For the first time, she realized the Archive wasn't just a parasite. It was patient. It was waiting. And it had found someone who might say yes.

THE FORBIDDEN WING had no doors, only an archway of bone, tall enough to dwarf a house. Its ribs curved inward like the fingers of a giant hand, and every step Asha took inside made the air heavier, thicker, as if the library were trying to compress her into silence.

The Curator waited in the centre of the chamber, a figure stitched from shadows and parchment. Its face was unreadable, a shifting mosaic of borrowed eyes and lips, voices humming beneath its skin. Its voice was not one voice at all, but thousands whispering in unison:

"You've come to choose."

The room was lined with towering shelves, but the books here didn't just breathe… they *watched*. Pages curled toward her like listening ears. The Curator circled her.

"You could stay," it said, *"live in this city with your memories restored, wrapped in a sweetness that never sours. Your friends will love you. You will forget that any bargain was ever offered."*

Then it leaned close, and its breath smelled of damp ink.

"Or…"

Its hand rose, long fingers blotched with ink stains, and pointed upward.

The shelves trembled.

"You can give yourself to me whole. I will collapse the Archive. Every captive memory will return to its owner. The city will be free. But… you will vanish from every mind. No one will remember you ever walked here."

The words struck her chest like cold water. She thought of Daro's face, the way his eyes had burned with recognition when she'd first whispered the coded fragments of her investigation. She thought of the others: the street vendors, the musicians, the children whose laughter was dimmed by the weight of stolen years. To free them meant becoming nothing.

Asha stepped forward, though her knees shook. "Take me whole," she said.

The Curator tilted its shifting head. *"And what of your precious words? They will rot with you in my gut."*

Asha smiled—not from bravery, but from the strange calm that comes when there's only one road left to walk. "No," she said. "Leave my words."

The Curator stilled, a hundred borrowed mouths going slack. *"Explain."*

Her voice shook, but each syllable landed like a pebble dropped into deep water.

"I've been writing for weeks. Not just in my journal but in the Archive's own margins, in the dust between shelves, in the condensation on the windows. A story hidden inside another story. I wrote the truth in metaphors Daro will understand. When I'm gone, the tale will find him. And when it does, the city will remember what it owes me."

A hiss passed through the shelves. The Curator regarded her like a puzzle with one missing piece.

"You think words can outlive you?"

"They already have," she said.

The Curator moved closer, its shadow spilling across her shoes like spilt ink. Then its mouth, or what became a mouth, opened impossibly wide.

The air turned black.

It wasn't teeth she felt, but *pages*, slicing through her, folding her into paragraphs, tearing her into strips of meaning. She felt herself breaking apart, the letters of her name scattering like startled birds. Pain, yes... but stranger than pain was the relief.

Somewhere above, the shelves began to shatter like glass. Scrolls unraveled mid-air, releasing bursts of colour that streaked toward the city beyond. She heard the cries of people remembering... first in confusion, then in joy, then in grief for all the years stolen.

The floor shook as the breathing of the Archive slowed... slowed... stopped.

The Curator's voice slipped into her ear one last time, almost tender: *"You will not be remembered."*

"I know," she whispered from the place between pages, "but my words will."

And then she was gone.

In the streets above, Daro looked up from the market square. A scrap of paper, curling with ash at the edges, landed in his hand. On it, a single sentence glimmered in fading ink:

The truth lives where the forgetting ends.

He understood.

And somewhere, in the hollowed silence of the Forbidden Wing, the last page turned.

THE CITY HAS RESUMED its rituals—the hum of barges moving between platforms, the salt-lanterns glowing at dusk —yet an invisible absence threads through Ndarama like a taut string.

Daro, older in the eyes though only weeks have passed, sits alone at a desk in the quietest corner of the Archives. The space smells of brine and pressed kelp-paper. Outside, the tide grumbles against the pylons.

He is sorting through new acquisitions when his hand rests on a manuscript wrapped in grey sea-cloth. No sender's name. No scribe's seal. He unties the knots. The handwriting is fluid yet unfamiliar, as though it is borrowed from a dream. It begins:

"Once, in a city that floated between tide and sky, there lived a girl who traded her name for the sea…"

Daro's throat tightens. Each sentence flows with the rhythm of waves, telling of a bargain struck to protect the memory of a people, a bargain so absolute that the girl's very name dissolved into foam. There are no dates, no citations. Just the story, breathing on the page as if it remembers itself.

Beyond the Archives, whispers rise. Traders pause mid-barter to murmur about the "storm" the Curator once warned of. Elders speak in half-remembered parables about bargains and tides.

No one mentions Asha. They cannot. Yet the sense of her lingers, a shape in the periphery, a syllable caught in the throat, a presence that feels like remembering a song's refrain without knowing its title.

In a distant wing of the library, a young apprentice, barely more than a child, turns to a blank page in her copying book. Her stylus hovers, uncertain. The page feels… expectant. Without understanding why, she writes four letters in a curling hand:

A S H A

The ink sinks into the paper like a seed into soil. She

stares at it, puzzled, certain she's never heard the name before. Still, a faint warmth blooms in her chest. She doesn't erase it.

THE CAMERA of the mind pulls back, past the glimmering domes and drifting markets of Ndarama, past the tide-harvest platforms and sail-lantern fleets. The city is quieter now, its waters reflecting the muted light of dusk. Yet beneath it, the ocean's surface stirs in irregular pulses, as though something vast and unseen is breathing. Far below, where the darkness deepens to a green-black, a single current curls toward the surface. The waves shiver against the pylons.

The storm is not here yet. But it is coming.

The Flavour of Memory

Alison Colwell

Tomasso spent three cramped days on the bus moving west as he tried to outrun his grief. When the bus stopped to pick up new passengers or drop off others, Tomasso read the headlines in the newspapers. They reported that police had arrested hundreds of rioters. Fires still ravaged parts of the city. For one sweltering July night in 1977, New York City had rioted, while Tomasso walked untouched through the devastation.

"It was an act of God," said the director of utilities.

"It was negligence," said the mayor, laying blame.

Tomasso bought stale sandwiches and bottles of Coke at the rest stop. He'd look around the town and wonder if he'd come far enough. He'd made promises that last night in the city, made a bargain with the goblins that had seemed like a good choice; but now, under the harsh fluorescent lights of the bus station's rest stop, he wasn't so sure.

Each time Tomasso checked his pockets for his ticket before re-boarding the bus, his fingers brushed the tattered exercise book that contained his recipes, written out in his slow, painstaking scrawl. The recipes were all he had left of the life he'd lived with his grandmother. They were the only things he wanted to hold on to as he fled in search of something new.

ON THE MORNING of the third day the bus pulled up to a low building and the driver turned off the engine. "End of the road, folks," the bus driver said as he swung open the door for the last time.

Tomasso clutched his backpack in his arms and followed the other passengers out onto the street. The pale blue sky seemed impossibly huge without skyscrapers biting at the edges. The unlikely looking palm trees bore no resemblance to the trees in Central Park. What would his Nonna have made of this town? As a young bride, she'd travelled from the old country to New York City, but then she'd folded herself into their neighbourhood and never left again. Tomasso shouldered his bag and straightened up. He would discover this new city for the two of them.

"Little Italy?" he asked the driver.

"Follow First Avenue that way," the man pointed back the way they'd come. "to West Cedar Street. Take a left and a few blocks down you'll hit India Street. You can't miss it."

After days on the bus, it felt good to stretch his legs. He started making a list in his head. Strong sweet coffee. Then a place to sleep. Only then could he think about how to realize the dream he'd bargained his life for.

The next day, Tomasso found a vacant pizzeria and spent almost all the money he had left putting down the first month's rent. He spent four days sanding tables and cleaning the kitchen, wiping down chairs and stacking wood for the oven. He painted "Nonna's Pizza" on the sign out front, and hoped she would've been proud of him, but he knew the deal he had taken would have outraged her. But she'd died, and he'd been alone and it had seemed like a good idea. Truthfully, it was the only idea that had kept him from the well of grief and the high bridge in the centre of the city that crazy night.

TOMASSO HAD WALKED AWAY from his grandmother's funeral a little over a week ago, not stopping till he had emerged unscathed at the Port Authority bus depot as dawn broke the following morning.

"Where do you want to go?" the attendant asked when he reached the front of the line. A fan sat unmoving on the desk behind her. Sweat beaded on her brow. It was 6:00 a.m. and the heat was already climbing. Lights flickered, and Tomasso heard the low chug of a diesel generator throbbing under "Hotel California" playing on the battery-operated radio.

"West," he said. He wanted to get as far as possible from the city and from the night market.

"Right. How far west?"

He pulled some bills from his pocket and pushed them towards the clerk. "How far will this get me?"

"Fifty bucks will get you a one-way ticket anywhere. You can go as far as San Diego. Lots of your kind there."

"Fine. San Diego, please."

"Bus will leave as soon as they've got the tunnels open. Don't go anywhere."

Tomasso nodded, tucked the ticket in his pocket. He was going west to make a fresh start.

WHEN HE FINISHED CLEANING the pizzeria, Tomasso hired Eva, who worked at the bodega next door. She brought her friend, Nick, to help with the dishes. Tomasso ordered sacks of flour, crates of San Marzano tomatoes, and gallons of buffalo milk.

Tomorrow he would open. He hung a sign in the window, then he went to work. He fetched the jar that he'd carried across the country from the flat above the shop. And for one moment, he wondered if he'd only imagined the magic it contained.

He twisted open the metal lid, then closed his eyes and breathed deeply. Felt his grandmother's hands resting over his as she showed him how to shape the soft dough. Smelled smoke from the wood oven. He felt the sorrow of her absence and the joy of her love.

Tomasso took out the smallest pinch of the yellow dust. It looked like saffron, the stamens of some impossible crocus that grew in the borderlands between our world and the next. It smelled like nostalgia. He dropped the pinch into a twist of paper, careful not to lose any threads, then screwed the lid back tightly onto the jar. Downstairs in his kitchen, he added the threads to the warm water, allowing it to infuse for a few minutes before he made the starter for the dough.

And while he waited, he closed his eyes and let the memories carry him away.

WHEN HE WAS EIGHT, Tommaso's Nonna had taught him how to make sauce. He'd stood on a stool beside her in the kitchen as she blanched the ripest San Marzano tomatoes in salt water, peeled them and crushed them by hand. She added torn basil leaves, their scent filling the small kitchen, and a drizzle of virgin olive oil.

Tommaso's mother had died when he was born, and he'd grown up sickly; all bony knees and poky elbows. His father had been ashamed of his delicate son and left him with his grandmother. Abandoned by both parents, he'd been an easy target for playground bullies and Tomasso had feigned sick more often than he attended school.

But with his grandmother, he'd only known love. He was the only link to the daughter she'd lost, and she was his everything. Their world had been small, wrapped up in the language of food, and it had been enough.

BY THE TIME the pizzeria had been open for a week, Tomasso had developed a routine. Rise at ten and stack wood, carry flour, make the mozzarella and sauce. Eva would arrive at four to set up the tables. Then she insisted he stop and drink a coffee with her, the strong sweet espresso made in the fancy machine she'd insisted they needed. At five, he unlocked the door and made pizza till nine. Then he'd lock the door, and while Eva and Nick were cleaning, he'd start the dough rising for the next day. Sleep. Repeat. There was comfort in the routine. The bands of grief around his chest loosened. Some afternoons he'd tell Eva stories about his Nonna, his memories not faded at all.

On that mad flight across the country, when he was staring out the windows as darkness rushed by, he'd wondered if he was doing the right thing in leaving so much behind. But now, with his hands in the dough, making the best pizza he knew how, with just that tiny pinch of magic, he knew he'd made the right choice. He was honouring his grandmother's legacy and sharing memories of love.

EACH NIGHT, as he added a pinch of the pollen to the starter, he breathed in the aroma and remembered his grandmother, and it hurt less.

He'd quit school when he was twelve. They'd needed the money. Nonna got him a job at Matteo's deli. He started out sweeping, then weighing out customers' cheese and sausage, but strangers made him anxious, so Matteo had moved him to the back and taught him to make cheese instead.

Tomasso loved stirring and kneading the cheese curds in the hot whey, drawing out the mass to create the elastic texture that characterized the best mozzarella. He shaped each fistful of curd into a tight ball, dropping it into the cold brine to set. It was skilled work and Tomasso surprised everyone by being good at it. Within a month, his bocconcini was as good as Matteo's. The mozzarella recipe had gone into his notebook alongside his Nonna's sauce recipe.

BY THE END of the first month, word of his pizza had spread. Patrons started lining up outside the building at ten in the morning. Tomasso drew the shutters and tried to focus on his work, ignoring the swell of voices outside and the way their desire pushed against the door. He knew they craved a bite of his pizza and the flood of memories it would unlock. He rolled his shoulders and got to work.

After six months, Eva needed two more staff to help her. From five until nine, customers filled every single seat in the restaurant. As soon as anyone vacated their table, someone else slipped into their still warm seat. Tomasso rarely left the building. He kept his head down and his eyes focused on the flames in his oven. Occasionally he'd look up and out across the small room, catch the moment a person took their first bite. They came because of the rumours, the hype, but he'd watch their eyes close as magic unfurled in their mouths and minds. He saw tears often. Heard the occasional unexpected bark of laughter. He saw astonished grace and reverence for what he'd created. Exquisite pizza garnished with memories of love, without any of the pain. His Nonna would have been proud.

EACH NIGHT, as he took a pinch from the jar, he tried not to notice that the level in the container was slowly dropping. One pinch at a time, but 365 pinches in a year, and then another year and another, and the huge jar was already only half full.

Each night, he breathed in memories.

When he turned fifteen, he'd already spent three years at the deli, and he wanted to try something new. Nonna got him a job at the neighbourhood bakery working for Signore Luca. For the first month, he carried sacks of superfine flour up from the basement to the kitchen. He'd peer into the great bowls of dough, left to rise for the morning bake.

After a month, Tomasso graduated from hauling sacks to kneading the dough. It differed from mozzarella, and his shoulders bunched under the strain, but he liked the work, liked the silken quality of the dough in his hands.

At the end of a shift, he could take a ball of dough home. Nonna taught him to flatten the discs, spin them in his palms to create the thin crust pizza she adored.

Luca's dough recipe had also gone into his notebook.

SOMETIMES IT SEEMS like only days have passed since he came to this strange city on the wrong coast and opened his pizzeria. Sometimes he surprises himself when he glimpses the man in the mirror, the one with fine flour caught in the lines around his jaw, and he realizes years have passed. Eva occasionally buys him fresh shirts, and only then does he notice that his old ones have holes. Without her friendship anchoring him to this place, he might have gotten lost in his memories. He notices the way she looks at him, and he knows she'd like more than friendship. But that wouldn't be fair. His life was not his own and he didn't want to hurt her.

Instead, he makes pizza.

One after the other, a continuous line of perfection. Presidents had changed while he served up pizza. There'd even been an actor in the White House, not that he cared about politics or the world outside. His only concern was finding perfect tomatoes or sourcing the finest flour. When he discovered Arizona shipped flour to Italy, he ordered it directly from the US farmers. His pizzas were better than anything he imagined growing up in the Bronx.

Nonna's was on the map. Literally. And, sometimes, late at night when he lay on his single bed above the pizzeria, beneath the grey wool blanket that scratched his skin, and the flour in his lungs made it hard to breathe, he wondered what it might have been like to lie next to someone, to open up his heart to the possibility of love again, but he'd made the choice not to let his Nonna go, and he couldn't drag anyone else into his bargain.

ON THAT LAST day in the city, the pain had been a physical weight bearing him down. She'd died, and he'd tried unsuccessfully to find his father, even though he hadn't seen him in years. In the end, Tomasso had stood alone beside her grave while the priest intoned the prayers. He'd wept with no one to judge him. When he left the graveyard, he'd just kept walking. He couldn't go back to the tiny apartment they'd shared. Without his Nonna, it was no longer home. Tomasso had still been walking, wrestling with his grief, when lightning ripped open the sky and the streetlights blinked out. Stores fell dark. The blackness had crashed across the city until it echoed.

In the summer heat and unfamiliar darkness, chaos erupted. Bricks crashed through windows. Buildings burst into columns of orange fire, and through it all, Tomasso had kept walking. Columns of smoke billowed between the buildings and the city roared like some monstrous beast waking from a nightmare. Shards of broken glass glittered on the pavement. A fire truck thundered by, siren wailing. The city exploded, but none of it touched him. No one saw him. Not the police with their nightsticks or the rioters with their hands full of stolen loot.

Finally, he'd stumbled into the middle of the Night Market. For years, Nonna had warned him to stay away from the goblin market. It sprung up unannounced and disappeared without a trace. It was a place where you could find the freshest tomatoes, ones to make a grown man weep, or truffles so fragrant a rich man might turn over every dollar in his pocket to own a single slice. Tomasso had never believed the stories.

Now he stopped and looked around. Rough canvas awnings stretched out from buildings. Oil lanterns hung from poles, casting deeper pockets of shadows. Fruit gleamed in the half light. Piles of lemons and tangy oranges. Baskets of plump cherries. Deep purple plums. Apricots as tender as a young girl's cheek. Crisp apples and tart quince. Behind the stalls, men peered at him curiously. Tomasso flinched when he realized they weren't men. Short and creased, with tufts of hair and pointed ears, bedecked with rings and dressed in peacock colors. Tomasso knew the old stories. He knew the dangers of Goblin wares.

"Come to buy?" shouted one of them.

"I have no coin," Tomasso lied.

"Coin, Pah!" said the man. "Come taste this," he held out a fig in his gnarled fingers and Tomasso could detect the sweet scent of vanilla and sunlight, with undertones of rich black earth. Tomasso had never believed her stories. He'd never listened to her warnings. He stepped closer and accepted the fig, felt it yield gently beneath the pressure of his fingertips, before he sunk his teeth into the skin, drew the flesh into his mouth, heedless of the juice running down his chin.

He looked up in surprise.

"It's perfect," he said. The little man beckoned him closer.

Tomasso stepped under the awning and looked at the fruits displayed. All were perfectly ripe, though it should be weeks before some were ready. Then he saw the large jar on a shelf at the back.

"What's that?" he asked.

The goblin smiled, his yellow eyes narrowing in a grin that was all teeth and cunning, but Tomasso didn't care. The jar called to him.

The man twisted off the lid and held it closer for Tomasso to inhale.

The weight of his grief lifted, and a wave of memory assaulted Tomasso. So real, he could taste it. His Nonna, the flour that slipped through his fingers, the security of falling into her embrace after running from the bullies of the schoolyard, the sweetness of the honeycomb she saved for him to enjoy on the worst days. It was moonlight on the basil on the windowsill, and tomatoes sun-warm from the vines on their tiny balcony. It was home.

"One pinch of this, and everyone will savour their sweetest memories with no pain. And their memories will never fade."

"How much?"

"For a pinch?"

"For the whole jar." Because suddenly, Tomasso knew what he had to do, knew that there was one last way he could honour her memory. He would make the food his Nonna had taught him to make. And season the meal with memories.

"The whole jar is impossible."

"Tell me," Tomasso insisted.

"How old are you?" the goblin asked.

"Twenty-one."

"A pinch might cost you a week, an ounce one month, but the whole jar, well, your life, would belong to me once the jar was empty."

"I don't care. Everyone's left. What do I want with endless years? I want to share the joy of memories without the pain."

The little man stuck out his hand, and they shook. Tomasso took the jar, wrapped it carefully in an old sweater before he tucked it into the backpack and ran back into the city as streaks of pink sky rose in the east.

"THERE'S a man asking for you at table six," said Eva.

"I'm busy," he said, his voice wheezing as he pulled in a breath.

"That's what I told him. But he won't order, and he won't move until he speaks to you. He says it's about a debt."

Tomasso set the dough he was holding down and stood up straight. He thought about the jar upstairs, the thin layer of pollen in the bottom.

"So fast." Tomasso sighed, glancing around his packed restaurant. He still knew grief, but it lived alongside the life he'd built. It no longer overwhelmed him. He looked at Eva and thought about the life he might have had if he'd made different choices. "Let me make him a pizza before I go speak to him."

Tomasso spun the dough between his fingers. The crust had to be perfect. He dusted the peel, stretched the dough across the surface, then ladled a spoonful of the freshest sauce on top. He sliced the buffalo mozzarella into rounds, arranged the pieces over the sauce, and tore up fresh basil to sprinkle on top, breathing deeply as the scent carried him back to his childhood. Then he drizzled on virgin olive oil and slid it into the great wood-fired oven. Tomasso watched the pizza carefully, shifted and spun it so that the dough swelled and cracked and singed perfectly. If this was going to be his last one, it would be his best.

Tomasso sliced the pizza into wedges, carried it to table six, and set it down before the little man. He sat down in the chair opposite.

"You found me," Tomasso said. Not that he'd been hiding, just that it was a long way from NYC to San Diego. He'd wondered if they'd bother.

"It was harder to get in than to find you," chuckled the goblin. The rings in his ears sparkled in the light of the candles. There must be some magic at work. None of his other customers were staring at the otherworldly visitor in their midst.

"Is it time?" Tomasso asked. Some days, the flour in his lungs meant he could barely breathe. He should have known his time was running out.

The goblin nodded. "Time to pay up."

"But first you must try my pizza. I insist," Tomasso said.

The goblin hesitated, but the aroma was already working on him, wrapping him in memories of cavernous halls lit by fireflies beneath tree roots in some forgotten place. He lifted a slice to his mouth and took a bite. Tomasso watched carefully. He saw the little man's eyes close in delight as the flavour of memories exploded in his mouth.

The goblin ate the second piece, then the third. He barely opened his eyes. When the plate was empty, he finally leaned back and looked at Tomasso in surprise.

"I'm ready now," said Tomasso.

The goblin shook his head slowly, uncertainty clouding his yellow eyes.

"We need to renegotiate," said the goblin. "Double or nothing."

Ten Years at the Gate

Marie-Hélène Lebeault

The house smelled like damp bark and chimney soot, the way it always had, but Sandra couldn't shake the feeling that something was watching her breathe. She'd driven up from Montreal that morning with a thermos of coffee gone cold and a box of garbage bags she wouldn't need—Betty's house was preserved like a museum, every doily in place, every book spine aligned.

The funeral had been three days ago. Small affair. Sandra had stood at the graveside counting the mourners: herself, the priest, Mrs. Gagnon from the post office, and two men in work clothes she didn't recognize. Betty, though a village resident for forty years, had remained private.

Kept watch, Sandra corrected herself, remembering something her grandmother had said during one of their rare phone calls. "Someone has to keep watch, *ma petite*. Even when they don't understand what they're watching for."

The kitchen was exactly as Sandra remembered: yellow linoleum, chipped but spotless; a wooden table scarred by decades of use; mason jars lined up like soldiers on open shelves. Betty's teacup sat on its saucer, a ring of Earl Grey stain at the bottom.

Sandra touched the rim. Still warm.

Her fingers jerked back, heart hammering. She'd been driving for three hours. Betty had been dead for a week.

In the living room, the grandfather clock had stopped at 3:17 a.m. The pantry held surprises: bags upon bags of salt, far more than one old woman could use. Rock salt, table salt, sea salt imported from the Gaspé. Some were opened and measured out in careful portions. Others were sealed but covered in dust, waiting.

That evening, Sandra called her supervisor at the school board. The conversation she'd been dreading for weeks. "I need more time. The house... there are complications."

"Sandra, we held your position through the stress leave, but the fall semester starts in three weeks. You were one of our best teachers. If you're not ready—"

"I know. Just another month to sort through Betty's things."

After hanging up, Sandra stared at her reflection in the black kitchen window. Thirty-eight years old, no husband, no children, just a career she'd fled when the panic attacks started. The AP Literature position was supposed to be her fresh start.

Now she was trapped in a house that breathed wrong, sorting through the possessions of a grandmother who'd collected salt like other people collected recipes.

That night, she dreamed of Betty sitting at the kitchen table, writing in a leather journal by lamplight. In the dream, Betty looked up and smiled—the sad, knowing

smile she'd worn at Sandra's mother's funeral fifteen years
ago. "You'll understand soon enough," dream-Betty said.

Sandra woke to find an envelope on the nightstand. Her
name written across it in Betty's careful script.

Inside: a brass key gone green with age, a hand-drawn
map of the woods, and a note in French that made her
blood go cold:

Si tu pars, assure-toi que la barrière soit fermée.

(If you leave, make sure the gate is shut.)

SANDRA FOUND THE JOURNAL, written in French, in
Betty's bedroom, tucked beneath old newspapers. The
leather cover was soft with handling, pages yellow and brittle. It read like a gardening log at first—notes about soil
pH, which herbs thrived in shade—but the entries grew
stranger:

*June 15th, 1985: Marie-Claire taught me the
old ways before she died. Mushroom rings appear
when the boundary weakens. Salted the perimeter,
but my hands shake more each year.*

*September 3rd, 1987: The Thibodeau boy has
the sight. Caught him drawing the marked trees,
symbols he's never seen. His mother thinks it's
imagination.*

*October 12th, 2015: Year thirty of watching.
The visitors grow bold. Found children's belongings*

by the eastern marker—things that haven't been reported missing yet. But they will be.

November 1st, 2023: The binding weakens. My blood is thin. Sandra will have to choose—stay and learn, or walk away and let them choose freely.

The journal trembled in Sandra's hands. She flipped to the sketches: twisted trees with faces in the bark, shadow figures with star-bright eyes, children walking toward a threshold that swallowed the world beyond.

They whispered to me first when I was nine, Betty had written. *The same age as Paul is now. They promised wonders beyond imagination. Marie-Claire pulled me back from the threshold, but sometimes I still hear them calling. Curiosity is their first weapon.*

The last entry, dated two weeks before Betty's death:

The door breathes faster. Cracks spread like an infection. If Sandra stays, she'll have ten years to learn what took me thirty to understand. If she leaves...

The entry ended there, ink scattered as if Betty's hand had been shaking.

———

AS SANDRA WALKED into town that afternoon, conversation drifted from the steps of the town hall.

"—third child in two years," Mrs. Gagnon was saying. "Paul Thibodeau's been gone for three weeks. Police from Sherbrooke came asking questions, but what can they find in those woods?"

"Paul was always strange," Mayor Dubois replied.

"Drew pictures of things that weren't there. His mother said he'd been having nightmares since he was small."

"Nightmares or visions?" Mrs. Gagnon shook her head. "Children didn't go missing when Betty was watching."

At the *dépanneur*, the clerk—a teenager with purple hair and watchful eyes—rang up Sandra's groceries in silence. Only as Sandra was leaving did the girl speak: "Betty always said I had the eye," she said abruptly, thumbing charcoal dust off her sketchbook. "Bought me supplies. Never told me what I was seeing, just that I saw it. I'm Amélie." The drawing made Sandra's breath catch: the woods behind Betty's house, rendered in charcoal. Trees marked with symbols, shadows moving independently, and in the centre, a crack in the air itself.

"The eye for what?"

"For seeing what wants to be seen." Amélie closed the sketchbook. "The dreams are getting stronger since she died. Something's calling my name from behind the trees. It sounds lonely."

Sandra left without responding, but she couldn't stop thinking about Paul Thibodeau. She'd taught middle school for twelve years—she knew the type. Sensitive, artistic, the kind who saw patterns in clouds and faces in tree bark.

The kind she'd once been herself.

THE MAP LED Sandra through marked trees, each carved or painted with symbols that seemed familiar and alien at once. Some looked like protection sigils; others resembled no alphabet she knew. Several had been scratched out, bark scarred with deep gouges that wept amber sap.

The woods were too quiet. No bird song, no rustling. Even her footsteps seemed muffled, as if the forest were holding its breath. The marked trees formed a rough circle with Betty's house at the centre. A boundary. A cage.

At the eastern edge, she found evidence that made her knees weak: a child's running shoe, blue with white stripes, tangled in brambles. The fabric was new, barely weathered. Size four. Paul was older. Bigger. This wasn't his.

As Sandra pulled the shoe free, the brambles parted to reveal a ring of mushrooms growing in perfect symmetry, their caps white as bone. The grass inside was brown and withered.

"Sandra."

Her name whispered soft as wind through leaves. She spun around, but the woods stretched empty. The voice had sounded like a child's—curious, not frightened.

"Who's there?"

Silence, then: "Don't leave us alone."

The voice came from everywhere, carried on still air that tasted of ozone and damp soil. Sandra clutched the child's shoe and ran, crashing through undergrowth that seemed to grab at her clothes.

That evening, she called the police in Sherbrooke. Sergeant Moreau was polite but unhelpful.

"We're aware of the Thibodeau case, *madame*. If you've found evidence, we can send someone to collect it."

"What about the other missing children?"

"I'm not aware of any other missing persons reports from that area. Sometimes children wander off. Sometimes they come back on their own."

Sandra hung up. Her fingers hovered over the screen as if waiting for another call that wouldn't come. She looked up Paul Thibodeau online and found a Facebook page that made her throat tight. The sketches were remarkable for a fifteen-year-old: dark trees with faces in bark, children walking with shadow figures, doors opening onto starlit voids.

The last post, dated three weeks ago: a charcoal drawing of the woods behind Betty's house, accurate down to the marked trees. In the centre, barely visible, was a crack in reality itself—a thin line of darkness that seemed to pulse.

The caption read: *They're waiting for someone to let them in.*

Scrolling back, Sandra found older drawings that made her hands shake. A nine-year-old girl standing in a similar forest, her face bright with wonder as shadowy figures beckoned. The girl looked exactly like Sandra had at that age.

She remembered now: the summer she'd spent with Betty, aged nine, after her parents' divorce. She'd wandered into those woods and seen things that made her mother drive up from Montreal the next morning, pale and shaking after a phone call.

"Some children see too much," her mother had said during the drive home. "We need to teach you to look away."

It had taken years, but Sandra had learned. Learned to dismiss shadows that moved wrong, to ignore whispers from empty rooms, to explain away every impossible thing until the impossible stopped trying to get her attention.

Staring at Paul's drawing of her younger self, she felt the weight of all she'd been made to forget.

SANDRA SPENT the next morning moving furniture in the basement, driven by a restlessness she couldn't name. Behind an old armoire, she found what she'd been seeking without knowing it: a section of stone wall that didn't match the rest of the foundation. The mortar was cracked, spider-webbing outward. When she pressed her palm against it, she could feel it breathing. In and out, slow as a sleeping giant, warm as human skin. Through the largest crack, darkness moved with purpose.

Betty's journal had more to say:

October 30th, 1975: Marie-Claire explained the bargain her grandmother had made in 1885, when the railroad brought strangers to our valley. The visitors had been seeping through for years— not evil, just other. Curious about our world, hungry for experiences that didn't exist on their side.

The disappearances started small. Livestock drained but unmarked. Children who sleepwalked into the woods and returned, speaking words in languages older than Latin. The town was ready to abandon the valley when Marie-Claire's grand- mother offered a different solution.

A pact. A watcher. One woman to guard the threshold. Ten years of service, then the choice to pass the burden on or let the boundary dissolve. I agreed when I was thirty-eight, Sandra's age now. I thought I was being noble. I didn't understand that some burdens choose their bearers.

When the time comes, gather ten stones from the creek, one for each year of watching. Mix Marie-Claire's ashes with salt from the pantry. The words will come when you need them, passed down through blood and bone.

Sandra ran her fingers along the breathing wall, feeling warmth pulse beneath her touch. The darkness pressed closer, not malevolent but intensely curious.

The visitors slip through in dreams first, Betty had written. *They whisper promises to the sensitive ones, artists and dreamers who haven't learned to ignore what they see. They offer wonders that would make our reality seem flat by comparison.*

They don't lie. The wonders are real. But consciousness that touches theirs is changed forever—not destroyed, just left half in their world, half in ours. Paul felt it first—the itch behind the eyes, the dreams that blurred the bark of trees into faces. Their kind always do. Artists don't guard against wonder; they open for it.

The last entry was barely legible:

The door cracks wider each night. I feel them pressing against the boundary, not with malice but with terrible patience. If Sandra walks away—and she should—something else will hold the threshold.

Something that doesn't care about keeping children safe.

Sandra backed away from the wall but she could still feel it breathing. In her pocket, her phone buzzed with a text from her supervisor: *Need your decision by Friday. The position won't wait longer.*

Friday was three days away.

THE STORM HIT without warning—one of those sudden Quebec squalls that turns the world sideways. Rain lashed the windows, and the power went out like breath. Sandra lit candles and tried to read, but every shadow seemed to move independently. The house itself seemed to shift in weight, as if whispering secrets to the wind. The basement wall pulsed in time with her heartbeat, cracks widening to reveal impossible geometries that shimmered like wounds in reality.

Around midnight, she looked out the kitchen window and saw him: Paul Thibodeau, standing at the edge of the woods. Barefoot, dressed as he had been in the last picture —jeans, hoodie, no jacket, like he'd meant to be gone only a moment. His eyes reflected not candlelight, but constellations that wheeled in patterns no astronomer had mapped.

Sandra grabbed a flashlight and ran outside, calling his name. He turned and walked into the trees, moving with the strange, flowing gait of someone learning to move in a reality with different rules. She followed through a corridor of wounded trees, their symbols scarred out, their sap glowing like old coals. The fog was so thick she could barely see her feet, but Paul's figure stayed just ahead, moving deeper into the circle.

"Paul, wait! Your parents are worried sick!"

He paused in a clearing she didn't recognize. The fog swirled around him, and when it parted, Sandra saw them: figures made of shadow and suggestion, tall as trees, thin as hunger. They filled the spaces between trees, crowded the edges of perception, pressed against the boundary with the weight of deep time.

Paul turned to her, and when he spoke, his voice echoed with harmonics that made her teeth ache.

"They didn't mean to hurt me, Miss Paquette. What they wanted was to understand." His smile pulled wide, unnatural, straining around syllables not meant for human speech. "To taste sunlight on skin. To hear the music in a child's laugh. To carry the weight of someone else's grief."

One of the shadow figures reached out with fingers like winter branches and touched Paul's face. Where it touched, he became translucent, more idea than flesh. But his eyes remained human, and in them Sandra saw not terror but wonder—the terrible, consuming wonder of a child shown the true shape of the universe.

"The door is opening," Paul whispered, his voice growing fainter. "Grand-mère Betty can't hold it anymore. Someone has to decide: keep watching, or let them choose freely."

The shadow figures turned their star-bright eyes toward Sandra, and she felt their curiosity like heat, like the world tilted toward them. They didn't speak, but she heard them anyway—voices that spoke to the folds in her mind where childhood dreams had once curled.

Come and see, they whispered. *Come and taste wonder. Come and learn what lies beyond the boundaries your kind have built.*

The temptation was overwhelming. Sandra took a step forward, drawn by the promise of experiencing something beyond the weight of ordinary grief. She thought of her classroom—rows of hollow eyes behind desks—and the day she'd crouched behind the filing cabinet, willing her lungs to obey.

Here was something larger. Something vast and strange and achingly beautiful.

No, she told herself, stopping at the edge of the mushroom ring. *This is how it starts. This is how they take the dreamers.*

"I can't," she said aloud, her voice breaking. "I can't leave them alone."

The fog thickened, and when it cleared, both Paul and the visitors were gone. Sandra stood alone; her flashlight beam cutting through empty air. But she could feel them watching from behind the veil, patient and hungry. Waiting for her decision.

SANDRA SPENT the next three days reading everything Betty had left—journals, notes, books with margins filled in three languages. The instructions were fragmented, like a recipe with half the ingredients missing.

On Thursday evening, her phone rang. Her supervisor. "Sandra, I need your answer. Are you coming back or not?"

Sandra stared at the phone, a tether to her old world. She could see it: her empty classroom at *Polyvalente* Jean-Baptiste-Meilleur, waiting for her return. Thirty desks arranged in neat rows. The poster of Gabrielle Roy she'd hung by the window. Marcus Dubois in the third row, the quiet kid who wrote poetry he was too shy to share, who reminded her why she'd become a teacher in the first place.

"I need to stay. There are things here I can't leave unfinished."

"I'm sorry to hear that."

Sandra hung up and walked to the basement, where the breathing wall waited. That night, she made her choice.

She gathered river stones from the creek—ten smooth rocks worn soft by centuries of water. In Betty's garden shed, she found salt and a coffee tin labeled *Cendres de Marie-Claire*. Her great-grandmother's ashes, saved for this moment.

In the basement, she arranged the stones in a circle around the breathing wall, feeling the weight of ritual settling into her bones. She mixed the salt and ash with her bare hands, feeling the grit of bone between her fingers, the whispered blessings of women who'd stood where she stood and made the same impossible choice.

The words came from somewhere deeper than memory.

"Par cette porte, nous gardons. Par ce sel, nous lions. Par ce sang, nous choisissons. Dix ans de veille, dix ans de garde, dix ans entre ce qui est et ce qui attend d'être."

(Through this door, we watch. Through this salt, we bind. Through this blood, we choose. Ten years of vigilance, ten years standing between past and future.)

She cut her palm with Betty's kitchen knife and let three drops fall onto the mixture. It hissed where her blood touched, and the wall's breathing slowed, deepened, steadied into the rhythm of deep sleep. The darkness receded. The visitors' voices faded to whispers, then to the barely perceptible hum of distant conversations.

Sandra pressed her bleeding palm against the stone and felt the binding settle into her bones like a second skeleton. "Ten years," she said to the empty basement. "I can do ten years."

The house exhaled around her, and for the first time since Betty's death, the breathing sounded peaceful.

SPRING CAME LATE THAT YEAR, but when it did, it came with a vengeance. Sandra planted Betty's garden with herbs that grew in careful patterns, vegetables that thrived despite poor soil, and flowers that bloomed in colours that didn't quite match seed catalogs.

She learned to read the signs: mushroom rings that appeared when the boundary weakened, animals avoiding certain paths, the way children's laughter sounded different when it came from the wrong direction. She walked the perimeter every morning with Betty's key around her neck, checking marked trees, renewing scratched symbols, listening for changes in the world's breathing.

Paul Thibodeau came home three weeks after the binding, thin and confused but alive. He remembered nothing about being gone, only strange dreams about walking through forests made of starlight. His sketches changed after that—instead of shadow figures and otherworldly landscapes, he drew ordinary things: his mother's hands, sunlight through kitchen windows, friends laughing at shared jokes. Beautiful things. Human things. Things that belonged entirely on this side.

Other children stopped disappearing. The town relaxed in ways Sandra felt rather than saw—longer pauses in conversations, easier smiles, the return of birdsong to the woods.

She took a job at the village school, teaching French and literature to children who looked at her with the same wary respect they'd once shown Betty. Some of the older ones—the artistic ones, the sensitive ones—would linger after class to ask careful questions about dreams and shadows. Sandra taught them what Betty could not: some doors were better left unopened, some curiosities better left unsatisfied.

"But what if we want to know?" Amélie asked one afternoon, her sketchbook open to a drawing of the marked trees, symbols transformed from warnings into invitations. Her eyes held the same dreamy intensity Sandra remembered from her own childhood. She saw doors where others saw only walls.

"Then you learn to want other things instead," Sandra replied carefully. "You learn to find wonder in the world that's already here. Trust me—there's enough magic in a sunset or a child's first word to last a lifetime."

Amélie nodded, but Sandra caught her staring toward the woods, eyes bright with dangerous curiosity. "Sometimes I think it would be beautiful," the girl said softly, "to see what they see. To know what they know."

She recognised the tilt of Amélie's gaze—the way it leaned just slightly beyond the world.

EVERY MORNING, Sandra walked the perimeter with Betty's key warm against her chest. The villagers nodded when she passed—respectfully, carefully, the way they'd once nodded to Betty.

Someone has to keep watch, their nods seemed to say. *Better you than no one at all.*

At night, Sandra wrote in Betty's journal:

Year one. The boundary holds. Paul sleeps peacefully in his own dreams. Amélie shows signs of the sight—I'll guide her carefully, teach her to look away before she sees too much.

On foggy nights, the whispers return—soft, persistent, like memory made voice. Not evil—I understand that now. Just other. Just curious about a world they can never fully enter.

Ten years feels like forever when you're twenty. At thirty-eight, with nothing left to lose, it feels like a gift. Time enough to learn what Betty knew, what women have always known about the price of keeping the world safe.

Sandra capped her pen and looked out at the woods, where fog rolled in from the border. In the distance, she could hear them calling—patient voices speaking in languages older than a human settlement in these hills. They could wait. They'd waited before.

Sandra would keep watch. Betty had. Marie-Claire too. One woman at the gate, holding the line between what is and what waits to cross.

The key around her neck pulsed with warmth, matching her heartbeat, and somewhere in the basement, the sealed door breathed in perfect time with her lungs. As if the house and its guardian had become one organism, one will, one choice made flesh and stone and stubborn, mortal love.

In the woods, something moved between the marked

trees—not quite shadow, not quite light, but something that existed in the spaces between definitions. It paused at the boundary, testing the strength of symbols carved in bark and written in blood, then withdrew.

But not far.

The fog thickened, and Sandra closed the journal, the pen warm in her hand, as if it too had been listening. Through the kitchen window, the marked trees swayed in windless air, and for just a moment—so brief she might have imagined it—the darkness between them pulsed like a slow, patient heartbeat.

The forest held its breath, waiting for the next dreamer to listen too closely, to ponder too deeply, to mistake curiosity for courage and step across the threshold into a wonder that never quite lets you come back.

The Fall that Dreams of Summer

Lynne Sargent

Elora is weeping over her husband's coffin when the Summer King arrives at the wake. She recognizes him instantly, like one might know an imaginary friend from childhood were they ever to suddenly appear. He is just as Elora always dreamed him: wrapped in a breeze and smelling of summer, with dark hair and darker eyes. The world outside the funeral home is damp with autumn mist but when he enters, it is as though he brings in a single, sharp ray of sun. A roguish grin paints his face exactly the right shade of danger. His hand is outstretched and waiting. Without words, he tells her what he wants. Him being here, like this, like a dream, tells her all she needs to know.

Back when she was the person to dream that kind of dream, this would have been a fantasy come true. Once upon a time, Elora would have drowned in his eyes as soon as he cast them upon her, pools black as the abyss though she would have pretended they were simply the darkest, richest chocolate. Now, she pauses a moment and looks to her husband, Ewan, lying there in the coffin, his own eyes closed and empty. Tears leak down her face not for the first time today, even as she takes the chance and strides out of the hall, past the receiving line towards the intruder. The line is flustered, then confused. She pays no attention to the murmurs.

She approaches the strange summer man and enters the warmth of his aura with deliberateness. She holds his gaze as though she is as tall as he and pauses for a moment before taking his hand. Then, without words, they both disappear.

She finds herself in a misty field alone, perhaps not too far from the funeral home, but then again, it could be very far indeed. The rain patters down gently, and a chill quickly lodges itself in her bones in the absence of the man's summer. She knows what he is. He is the king of the summer court, of eternal summer, Lord of Dreams and any other activities that might happen while nestled in a bower. Her memory has not failed; she remembers her long year of searching for him, for his court. And yet, why has he come now, so many years later?

She is transported back to when she was a wayfaring twenty-something, searching the hidden corners of the world for a single, solitary speck of magic, back before she met Ewan. And yet, here she is again, stuck on a barren moor, chaste, alone, wanting. She tries not to think about Ewan; it is still too fresh. But this? The grief of all the promise of wonder that she never found? That fancy, that dream, that desperate belief she thought was gone from her, and yet, there he was, and now here she is, and she knows it was no dream that took her from that place of grief to this emerging adventure.

It is the faery ball of her dreams; her wedding night

done over again. The fey dance in masks under the moon, decked in satin and sparkles and cobwebs and diaphanous chiffons, and in nothing but their own skins. They dance in a hundred different ways: some waltz with partners, some move all on their own, twisting and turning and completing gymnastic feats, some have their limbs entwined with another's as though glued, threading their arms and legs in loops, like a children's puzzle game embodied, though the goal does not seem to be to untangle themselves. The band plays at the edge of the revels on instruments she has never seen before; some beautiful, some grotesque. There is a harp made of guts and bone, a tambourine of fireflies, panpipes carved from pearl. A feast of hors d'oeuvres is laid out on a hundred twinkling plates floating just above the heads of the guests. In the corners, there are fountains of what smells like champagne and looks like starlight with delicate crystalline cups ringing the lip, waiting to be filled. Elora does not know if she can dance after the trek, but the last week has taught her all she ever needed to know about drinking.

Reckless, she takes a cup and dunks it in the fountain, bringing it back up to her lips in one fluid motion and downs it in one swallow. Just as soon as the last drop has crossed her lips, the Summer King appears before her. She licks her lips, taking in the last drop. It is a pointed gesture, but not lascivious. It says, *you can't get rid of me now.*

He raises an eyebrow, then smiles. "I see you have found our revels. Let me dress you for the occasion."

As the dress substantiates around her, it is as though a new skin attaches itself to her along with it. It is soft and silken against her now smooth skin, equally unwrinkled. It is midnight blue with a chiffon cape dappled in stars. The neckline is high and even, elegant as it falls across shoulders no longer hunched with gravity's daily erosion of her posture. It is a miracle, a kindness that she would not have expected so soon, but then again, she thinks to herself, *Faery cannot abide even the barest hint of death.*

"Better," he says, sizing her up, pausing to observe.

She is too bewildered to notice the pause, to notice how the world around her stops as he does, as though all the court is waiting for him to make a choice. Finally, he does.

"Would you like to dance?" he invites, his gaze magnetic on hers as he sweeps into a perfect bow.

She starts to protest, to remind him and herself that her bones are old, that this is a dream gone far past its expiry date, but the music starts and it fills her soul, animating her limbs. It has been so long since she danced. Ewan was always eager, but as they aged it seemed less safe, and then the fall, and then his hip, and then her arthritis. But these cares, too, are pushed out by the music. She takes his hand and he sweeps her away. She is a puppet in his arms, spinning this way and that. She is young. She is the belle of the ball. She is drunk on starlight and the freedom of movement, high on misspent youth.

"What is it like, to be the king of fey?" she asks as they whirl.

"Unimaginable, for a mortal. Even one with an imagination such as yours. But I imagine it is very like being any other kind of king. My first duty is to my people. My own desires are secondary." For a moment, his gaze flicks past her shoulder as though to find someone else in the crowd. Then, after a breath, he redoubles his efforts in the dance and they go too far for her to speak any more. After what seems like hours, they slow, and she tries again.

"Do I get to stay?" she asks. She cannot imagine going back to that world where Ewan is not. He is not here either, but he never was here, and that makes all the difference.

"Perhaps," he says, pausing; then, as if remembering himself, he pulls her close once more and whispers in her ear, "finding us was only the first task."

A dark frisson of excitement runs through her. To have a task, a challenge. To be young and hungry and needing to prove something. He stays close, his breath heavy and wet and his hands all too large and hot on her body. As he pulls her closer, all she can think about is Ewan's hands, frail in the last few years, and how she cannot imagine anyone else's hands holding her like his did. She shudders in sudden disgust, leaning away as much as she can while still trapped by his hand on her shoulder blade. She creates space in their frame, as though she can make him feel her discomfort if she subjects him to the same, but she is not so youthful to think that is how men have ever worked. Still, she remembers this game. She whispers back into his ear, tongue wet, "Then get me another drink and tell me what comes next."

He steps back, his eyes teasing intent. "I would, but alas, the sun rises on our revels." He gestures to the dawn behind him. "To find me again, you must believe. A true belief. One which can withstand the light of day. Perhaps it will not be so hard this time." With that, he disappears into a black swirl that looks like a pool of oil being slowly dissolved by the pink sunrise.

The faery world fades around her too, and she is transported once more. She finds herself at Ewan's grave, the sun harsher here, as though she has caught up with it. The flowers set against his headstone already wilt. Her purse is beside the headstone and she picks it up, reaching in to find her cellphone. There are a dozen texts from her younger sister, Marie, and two from her niece, Jean, asking where she'd run off to, if she was okay.

She thinks about texting back, then decides against it. Marie has already proposed the idea of her going into a home; it hadn't even taken two days after Ewan had passed. She'd said "I know you're competent, but you never know what could happen. You could have an accident. Just take a little slip, or God forbid, have a stroke. It's just not safe for the elderly to live alone. This is why we have children! But of course, you don't. I just... I would never be able to forgive myself if..." and on and on it had gone. How Marie would balk if she knew of Elora's adventures last night, but then again, Marie had always been judgmental of Elora's "lifestyle," as she called it.

The Summer King had asked her to believe in him— and she will.

She thinks back to that summer, so long ago now. She sees the fireflies, the nettles, remembers the words she so lovingly scribed in her journal. She thinks of her descriptions of the fields, of getting rid of Tim and finding Ewan and everything else in between, and how desperately she had wanted faery. She thinks of the long hikes she took by herself, of all she put up with so that Tim could help with the travel costs, because she so needed to see if this was all there was in the world or if she could find them—the hidden world—and leave this all behind instead. She remembers each detail, each clue, the toadstools there one day and gone the next. The strains of music in the mountain that she could never quite get close enough to.

Elora returns home and waits until sunset to go in

search of the faery court. She puts on the dress she wore for her 40th with Ewan: the simple purple velvet wrap, now an old dress on a young woman. She takes the bus to the edge of the city, but with the city turning into night, she fits in with all the other young folk heading to the bars and the concerts and the restaurants. The bus empties as it completes the route, and at the last stop, the driver asks if she's sure she's getting off at the right place. It is a stop on the far outskirts of the city, just before where the road turns into nothing but a winding, single lane populated by cows more than cars. Elora replies that yes, she is at the right place and gets off the bus.

As the bus drives away, she moves off the road toward the great stone fences that trace the landscape here. She hops the fence and begins her trek across the fields. She is still an old widow alone, kept companion only by the rain and the smell of salt in the air.

She asks herself if she is abandoning Ewan, but she cannot be, for he is already gone. So, she chooses the quest and begins walking. She sets off in search of the nettles, the mounds, the rings of toadstools, the standing stones, the place the dance is being held, the dance that she has finally been invited to join.

The damp ground is hard on an old woman's bones. Elora twists her ankle in the mushy muck and scrapes herself on brambles as she falls. Yet, she pushes herself to her feet and keeps going. What is a twinge in one ankle when it seems that her entire skeleton is a kaleidoscope of small aches and wearinesses?

The sky goes dark and the clouds refuse to let the stars twinkle through. She is alone, as alone as she has been this last week without Ewan, but it is a different kind of loneli-

ness. It does not have the same quality as her standing solitary, the receiver of grief and condolence in equal measure
at the wake. It is not the same as their bed, left empty after
he went to the hospital never to return—though she didn't
know it at the time. It is the final kind of lonely, the kind
where she could die and no one would know, and perhaps,
that would be a peace. She imagines the ghost of Ewan's
hand in hers, and she trods onward. He would understand
this dream. If he were here, he would be with her, he would
have run through that door at her side. She would have had
one hand in his and one in the Summer King's and they
would have gone to this land together. She hears his voice
whisper in her ear as though he had come with her: "Go
on, my love."

She pants and heaves. Her bones creak. The knee she
dislocated as a child begins to click with every step. She
finds a stick to lean on. There will be no dancing for her
when she arrives unless they decide to put her on a palan-
quin and carry her around as part of the revels.

Finally, after what seems like hours, like longer than
night can even go on, she sees a hill in the distance. She
hobbles toward it, faster now, reinvigorated, hungry. Now
she goes on, not simply so that she will not die out here of a
chill or otherwise. She goes on because she *wants* it.

She begins to hear the sound of a frenzied, discordant,
rapturous tune. She falls into the music's beats and loses
track of her own feet. The melody colonizes her hips, then
her shoulders, and then finally her hands. She is lilting and
leaning and flicking this way and that. She finds her eyes
closing and just as she begins to spin, the Summer King's
arms catch her, and suddenly his court is all around.

It is a different kind of party tonight, a darker one.

Though it is autumn, the bodies swirling around smell like the rot at the end of summer before the leaves finish falling and the cold can begin to sterilize the earth. The dancing is rapturous and it seems as though the first song goes on for an age. As the music rises further, the Summer King swoops her down into a low dip and kisses her full on the mouth. He himself smells musky, like he has been rutting the whole time she has been away and couldn't be bothered to wash. It would disgust her if she thought this was a courtship. On second thought, it still disgusts her, since he must think it is.

That disgust takes over once again as Ewan and all the kisses they shared flash in her mind. She pushes the king away as though she can push away all the memories, all the hurt that they are over, along with him. With the force of it all, she heaves herself up even as she knocks him down hard, their positions reversing, only she is not there to catch him at the bottom and he falls to the ground. The music jars to a stop. The faery creatures whirl around to face Elora; horns and feather and ethereal tendrils all stand on edge, and all are focused in her direction.

One of the closest men, if that is even the right word to call him, approaches swiftly. His body seems to be made from the rocks that live under the streaming of a waterfall. Mist sprays off of him and he is slick and mossy. His mouth is more like a gaping geode than anything else. As everyone, including Elora, stands stunned, he moves towards her and slaps her, hard. As hard as Tim had, the night she'd left him. "You dare disrespect our king so?" he asks in a crashing, hard, voice.

Elora doesn't even think. She hits him back, finding the strength in her renewed bones overriding any fear. She is pure reaction.

The man inflates with rage. He winds up, readying himself to strike again. The crowd eggs him on with gleeful, predatory smiles.

The Summer King scrambles to his feet, recovering his prior perfection with a wave of his hand through his hair. He places a hand on the waterfall golem's arm.

"Stop, Carriston," he says. "It matters not. You know she cannot hurt me."

Carriston kisses his king's cheek and whispers in his ear, though it is loud enough for the entire court to hear. "It is disrespectful of a future consort. You know, if I…" he trails off, his eyes full and gleaming as he stares at the Summer King. It is clearly a conversation that they have had before.

"Hey. Slow down," Elora interrupts. "I don't want to be anyone's consort." She leaves off the *sorry I wasn't clear earlier*. She is past apologizing for such things.

The Summer King whirls to face her, his expression equal parts bewilderment and rage. "Then why did you come with me? Why did we dance? Your husband is gone now. You owe him no further bond!" Then he drops his voice, whispers, as if to himself. "We were sure that this time… and now, there is so little time left."

"I wanted an escape from our life. From the memories, the pain of it all," Elora retorts, thinking to herself, *not that that worked particularly well*. "I didn't want a new husband! I wanted distraction and purpose again, even if it was just in the frivolity of the next dance. I wanted something more than the nothing that was left."

Carriston snorts, disdainful "And a good thing too, since you'll never make it back properly with how you hammered back our drink last night." The crowd titters.

A triad of women who look like they are made of

spiderwebs approach, and they bow before the king. "We will take her off your hands, your highness," one of them clacks. "We will keep her from insulting your royal personage until it is time." The speaker licks her lips while the others stare openly at Elora, salivating.

"You know she must be willing," the Summer King replies. "Ah! It is no good. There is no time. Who will serve the next cycle?"

"Serve as what?" Elora asks

"As our human queen and tithe? What else, child?" he mutters the word 'child' like it is a curse, then explains as though she is one anyway. "This is the pattern we are forced to live by. This is the way the story is meant to play out: you are supposed to become my queen consort after a whirlwind courtship. You would then serve for a few years, fall in love with my lands, and volunteer as tithe when the time comes. Every twenty-one years this happens, every generation, every three times seven."

"But I am already in love with your lands! That is why I am here. My own, what little they held once, have no joy for me now. This is the only place since Ewan went into the hospital where I have not ached, where the drink doesn't leave me more wounded in the morning than I was before I turned to it in the first place. The music here is the only thing that can burn away the mist of wanting for his arms that seems to haunt my very bones." At this, Elora bursts into tears and the crowd falls deathly silent.

"I see," says the king. Carriston holds his arm tight. The king seems unsure of what to do with this all too human expression of feeling, with the dislogic of missing, of grief that cannot be filled by just anything. How could he know what to do? The fey need humans to remind them of such things.

Elora sits with them for a time and explains love. She tells them how it can be both a promise, and simultaneously, something that asks for nothing in return but the existence of the object of the love. She tells them how she has long loved both Ewan and the land of fey, how they gave her a reason for living when she thought this world beyond meaning. How they still do.

"So," the king begins again, but he does not need to finish his question.

"Yes," Elora answers. "I will be your willing tithe when the time comes. I will bind myself to your lands and do whatever else is required, but I will not be your consort, and I will not give my body to any creature or person in your lands."

Now the crowd cries too, leaking various fluids in small rivulets from open spaces. It is a quiet affair. Then the king, before all his court, approaches the human woman and softly whispers, "May I embrace you as a hero? As a friend?"

Elora nods quietly, and they embrace.

The days after that fateful ball are easier, but harder too. There is so much to see in the lands of fey, but it is not the same without Ewan. The sunset fields and cloud trees are a joy and a longing. The dryad villages are an adventure of a lifetime, but the fey will not climb through the lofty jungle-gym bower with her as Ewan would have. Instead they flit, or fly, or project, not understanding the fulfillment that comes with exertion, in an adventure that lives firmly in the steps taken by your feet.

It is five years until the beast comes, and the tithe must

be paid. Elora is an old woman now, just on the cusp of eighty, though you would not know it from looking at her... and she is ready. She thinks about returning to Jean and Marie, to say goodbye, but she has already been gone so long it seems cruel to reopen old wounds.

The Summer King walks her to the cave where the monster waits and kisses her chastely on the cheek, thanking her once more.

Elora spends her last moments thinking of Ewan. Not about the river where they met, but the day she properly chose him, the day that they truly began. It had been a week after the first time, and she was leaving a bar to go out into the fields where she had spotted a bonfire in the distance. As she walked, she saw Ewan, his back receding down a twisting alley heading deeper into the city, away from the fire and the strange music that had previously beckoned her. She remembers how, seeing him, she had made the choice to turn away from the hot light and into the colder darkness and cobblestones, and she had followed him.

True Ink

Jesse Scoble

The hiss of the autoclave filled the small parlor, and the sharp tang of rubbing alcohol mingled with the haze of incense. The artist peered at their canvas. They dabbed at the ink with a paper towel. The girl's back was smooth and fair, and her skin held a faint scent of pepper and black raspberries. The needle bit into flesh and the girl curled her lips in a grimace, failing to stifle a small, "Ow!"

"It hurts less with each tattoo," Jo said, relaxing the needle for a second.

"Really?" the girl asked.

"No, not really, but I'll be done soon." They both laughed a little, until Jo went back to work.

The parlor, True Ink, was unusual in several ways. Jo's partner, Scout, did most of the walk-ins, handling the run-of-the-mill art. Jo, on the other hand, took customers only by appointment. And while Scout was good—as good as any in the city—Jo was a magician with a needle.

Jo refused to do "flash," the carbon copy images pulled out of a thousand tattoo magazines. They solely did personalized work and had earned a name amidst the culture. A crazy eccentric who lost money despite charging outrageous prices due to expensive materials and limited work, a proud and arrogant artist who could make a fortune if they turned commercial—but a legend, nevertheless.

The back station was curtained off for privacy. Robbie Roberston's reedy, haunting voice sang out of Jo's small speaker as they focused on the work. "*Catch the blue train, to places never seen before, look for me, somewhere down the crazy river.*"

Scout was out of town this weekend visiting family in Chicoutimi, and Jo was running the shop alone. Which was fine with them, as they only had one appointment this evening: Cassie Waters, a rich girl from the right side of the tracks, but who had a good heart despite those privileges.

They had been working for three hours with no distractions. So Jo was a little startled to hear the door chime as they put the last touches on Cassie's art: a dragonfly swooping over the hint of a river across her right shoulder. With Jo's attention distracted, the dragonfly's wings started to vibrate as if it were going to fly right off Cassie's back. Jo bit their lip and murmured, "No, no, you're not going anywhere." With a light touch of the needle, the art settled down.

"Hmmm?" Cassie asked.

"Nothing," Jo said, as the front door banged shut. "We're done for tonight. Stay here while I see what's up." Cassie nodded as Jo slipped out from behind the curtain into the heart of the store.

A pair of huge bruisers were giving the place a hard look.

"Sorry guys, we're closed for tonight," Jo's voice was

steady, but at 5'2" in combat boots, they felt like an insect in front of these behemoths. The smaller one must have been 6'8", while the other was a half-head taller.

"Door was open." The behemoth spoke in a voice that sounded like a cleaver being sharpened on a grinding stone. He was wearing wraparound shades despite the hour, and what Jo could see of his pale skin was sallow and pock-marked. A sweat and salt-stained tee-shirt stretched tight over his massive frame. He snarled. Cracked lips pulled back to reveal nicotine painted teeth. "So you open, yeah?"

Jo couldn't really argue with that.

Jo took a deep breath as the shorter one picked up a delicate tattoo machine in a meaty paw. His face was hidden beneath waves of white dreads. Jo anxiously ran a hand through their short spiky-blonde hair as Dreadlocks *sniffed* the tool.

"Well, I'm closed for the night. No more customers."

"No problem," the big one barked. He yanked his black tee-shirt down by the collar, and Jo could make out dark, ugly brands on his neck. The flesh was puckered and scarred. "These real strong symbols," he said, letting the shirt snap back into place. His English was broken and accented, but Jo couldn't place it. Possibly Eastern European. Possibly much farther afield. "Don't want you silly pictures." He gestured at the ink visible on Jo's arms, an armband of Ultima runes on their left bicep, and a styl-ized triple-lightning bolt on their right inner forearm.

Then, almost ignoring Jo, he craned his neck to scan the shop. "Looking for a baby crow."

"Smells like crows," Dreadlocks growled, his nose poking through his curtain of hair.

A crow? Jo thought, then realized he must mean one of

the local street kids, who called themselves the Queen Street Crows. Which probably made these two Driftwood Kryptic, a much nastier gang with a bloody reputation. "Aren't you boys a little far south? This isn't your neigh-bourhood," Jo said, regretting the words almost as soon as they left their mouth. Scout was always telling Jo to behave and play nice, that being too honest would one day get them into a fix they couldn't talk their way out of.

Dreadlocks carelessly tossed the tattoo machine onto a table and Jo winced as something snapped. "See this?" he growled, spinning to show off the back of his leather jacket. It was emblazoned with the Driftwood stamp under the image of a bull's skull. "Driftwood Kryptic own *every* street. We grind everybody else up!" That was probably true, even if three-quarters of their vicious acts were urban legend.

"Sure thing," Jo said. "I don't want any problems."

"Then give us baby crow," the first one snapped.

Jo thought about Cassie for a second. Not that they would ever have given her up, but regardless, Cassie wasn't a crow of any sort. The girl's sign was a dragonfly, swift and pure, clear as a mountain stream.

"Look boys," Jo raised themself up to their full height—they only barely crested the big one's gut but never mind—and locked gazes. "There aren't any crows here. Baby or otherwise. So get the hell out."

The big one's lips curled back, baring his yellow teeth.

Dreadlocks stepped towards Jo and snarled, "Watch how you talk. Nobody and no one speak to Shark Face like that," he said, indicating his companion.

"Yeah? And what's your name, you tubby hairball?"

"White Fang," he spat.

"Jack London...? Really?" Not giving him a chance to

answer, Jo rolled on, their voice gaining strength with every short burst.

"Okay, you fish heads, listen up.

"There are no crows here.

"This is my place, not yours.

"You have no claim here, so you don't have to go home, but you do have to get the hell out." Although Jo never raised their volume to even a shout, by the time they finished speaking it was like the store was being rocked by thunderheads.

The two thugs winced against the barrage of words.

"We leave," Shark Face spat, "but you find crow, you give to us, or Driftwood Kryptic rip the pictures from your skinny body."

As soon as they left, slamming the door so hard Jo was sure the hinges would tear off, Jo was back to Cassie's side.

"You okay?" the girl asked Jo, relief flooding her voice.

"Yeah. These guys have the brainpower of goldfish. Shamu-sized goldfish mind, but... Anyway, they aren't looking for me or you. Still, I bet they'll hang around on the street for a bit, searching for..." *who are they after, and why?* Jo wondered, "...for whoever," they concluded lamely. "We're done for tonight anyway. Let's get you cleaned up and off home. Probably through the back alley."

"You're going to stay here?" Cassie asked, wide-eyed.

"For a little while, to make sure they don't try anything. Don't worry. I won't do anything stupid." *Scout would say staying here alone is stupid. Shut up!*

"Okay. We'll do the colours soon?" Cassie asked as Jo cleaned the area and applied a disinfectant spray. It stung, but Cassie didn't complain. Then Jo covered the area with a clear adhesive wrap.

"Yup. I've got some new recipes that I think are going to rock your world. Give me a call in three weeks when you're healed up."

After Cassie got dressed, Jo led her into the small office that doubled as a supply room, which had a door that exited onto the alley that ran between Queen and Adelaide streets. Cassie left with a final "goodbye" and a "be careful" hug. *She's a sweetie.* Jo closed and locked the door, *but too innocent for these streets.* Jo considered calling Seth or Monkeybird to see if they could swing by, but remembered they were in Vegas for the weekend. Then all thoughts vanished as Jo caught a whiff of cloves. They paused at the inner door and turned, scanning the cramped office.

A scratched desk and a faded leather chair took up a large part of the room. Much of the rest was filled with stacked boxes of needles, ink, and sterilization supplies. A small fridge and assorted knickknacks, like the Manchester U pendant that decorated one wall and a long-expired Too-Much-Coffee Man calendar on another, took up the rest. Jo sniffed again and slowly walked over to the desk. The top was covered in Scout's accounting books, stained coffee mugs, and a plush moose that was shockingly male. Jo stepped behind the desk and yanked the chair out.

Crouched beneath it was a tiny figure curled inside some sort of giant wrap. All Jo could make out was a young child's face. The child's pale skin was made even whiter by huge rings of mascara encircling the eyes. Jo wasn't sure if it was a boy or girl underneath the wild hair, spiky with sweat and black dye, but he or she was clutching a clove cigarette.

"Come out of there," Jo commanded, and reluctantly the child climbed out and stood defiantly in front of them, still wrapped in what appeared to be an enormous black tent.

"What's your name, kid?"

"Call me Cowboy." *Boy*, Jo realized.

"Somehow, I don't think so. You're a bit young to be part of a gang, eh?" Jo placed him at no older than thirteen, probably younger.

"Shut your hole! Tonight I became a man and earned my name!" he squeaked, trying to sound defiant.

"Watch your mouth," Jo snapped. The boy took a small step back and dropped his smoke before he remembered to be bold. He ground the cigarette out with his heel and then puffed out his chest.

"I earned my name," he repeated and hurled the garment on the floor with as much flourish as he could muster under its heavy weight.

"What's this?" Jo asked.

"I counted coup." He suddenly smiled like a boy who had cut off his sleeping sister's hair.

"You what?" Jo bent down to look at the object. It was an oversized leather coat. "What the hell is counting coup?"

"I watched the enemy and killed him, but bloodlessly." He was giddy with adrenaline and probably sugar, Jo surmised. Jo lifted the jacket off the ground and let out a sharp breath when they saw the bull's skull on the back—this belonged to one of the Driftwood Kryptic thugs. *The big one*, she thought. "I counted coup," he repeated, "like the Incas did in Mexico."

"I think you mean the Aztecs," Jo said, off-handedly, "but also not the Aztecs. Lord, kid, it was the indigenous of the Great Plains that counted coup. Not the Aztecs."

"Whatever. Now I'm a Queen Street…"

"Baby crow," Jo muttered under their breath, then, "Oh Lord."

He looked so smug, Jo thought. "So you find the biggest bruiser in town, steal something he'd kill for, and run and hide."

"No, you have to take it back to the Rookery," the boy spoke solemnly.

"What's the Rookery?"

"Our house. The Queen Street Crows."

Jo pointedly looked around the office, then at him. "And you've already done this?"

He didn't look so smug all of a sudden. "No..."

"So...what's your name, kid?"

He mumbled so quietly Jo forced him to repeat it. "Adam."

"Okay, Adam, I'm Jo. What's your plan?"

Adam heaved the jacket up off the floor and did his best to fold it in his arms. "I wait for those jacknecks to leave, then I take this to the Rookery."

"I don't think they're going to go unless you leave first. And while they probably won't try anything with me around, if I leave you here, they're going to tear this place apart. Not that I'd leave you here, but I don't want to spend the night in the shop, and I don't want to see you dead."

"Doesn't matter," Adam said. "I need to get to the Rookery before dawn." He peered over Jo's shoulder into the main part of the shop, as if expecting to hear the front window smash at any moment. "But I already called the Crows for help so they'll be here s-soon," he said, trying to fill his voice with confidence, but a slight chatter gave it away.

"Scout goes away for a night and I get the studio caught

in a gang war. C'mon," Jo grabbed Adam by the arm. "Leave the jacket on the desk and let's check the street."

The front of the store had a large stained-glass window that looked onto Queen Street. Jo dimmed the front lights to see the night. Peering up and down the street, they spotted Shark Face across the road. He leaned on a huge Harley, the air around him thick with cigar smoke.

"Is it clear?" Adam asked, hanging back.

"Clear as diesel fumes," Jo muttered.

"What?" Adam asked.

"No, not clear at all. Shamu is watching the front door, and I'd bet your bodkin his skeevy buddy is lurking in the alley," Jo said, irritation creeping into their voice. "How long 'till your pals show up?"

Adam pulled a cellphone from his pocket and glanced at it. No messages. "Uh, I'm not sure. Soon, I bet."

"What did they say?" Jo cupped their hand against the glass to watch Shark Face more clearly. His eyes constantly roamed the street, never resting.

"Um, they said they'd tell the Crow King, and he'd decide."

"The Crow King?"

"Me."

The new voice caused Jo to spin round, tense and furious at having another trespasser in their space.

The speaker was another boy, but unlike Adam who was trying to look older than his years, this youth had a maturity about him. Although he appeared to be sixteen at most, his grey eyes were fathomless, like an endlessly cloud-covered sky. Wild, inky hair formed a rough halo around his pretty face.

"Where the hell did you come from?" Jo demanded.

"The window was open," the tall boy said, casting a glance toward a small window set up high over the back door. While it was, in fact, open, he'd have to be some kind of contortionist to fit through it. Jo scowled at him. "You can call me Christian. Or the Crow King. Whatever you prefer," the boy said.

"Thank you for coming so quickly!" Adam's expression was reverential. "Where are the others?" he asked, moving to stand next to Christian. Both boys were dressed all in black, but while Adam looked like he'd gotten into his older sister's hand-me-downs, Christian's tee-shirt and jeans screamed money.

Jo was surprised to see Christian's distain. "Others? What others?"

"I told Domino that I counted coup—I stole the colours from the leader of Driftwood Kryptic— but I had to hide out here..." Adam trailed off as Christian twisted his head to the side, the way a bird stares at something it can't quite understand. Christian cocked his head one way, then the other. The silence stretched out painfully. Finally, Jo couldn't take it anymore.

"Lord. What the kid is asking, *Christian*, is what's your plan to get him out of here in one piece?"

Christian turned his puzzled gaze on Jo. "Why would I do that?"

"Uh, because the bruisers outside will, perhaps literally, tear him apart. And he's one of your group."

"Not yet, he isn't."

"I—" Adam started.

"Didn't he do your stupid challenge thing already?" Jo interrupted.

Adam dashed into the back to grab the jacket and

dragged it to the front room. "See, Christian, I did it!" His enthusiasm was cut short by Christian's frigid expression. The room felt like the temperature had dropped ten degrees.

"You have *not* successfully counted coup yet."

"I'm not sure how I feel about you appropriating that term," Jo said, but Adam and Christian ignored them.

"I know I have to get back to the Rookery, but I thought—"

"Find the enemy. Kill him bloodlessly. Return with the prize before the night breaks…"

"But it's still—" Adam tried to interrupt, but Christian spoke over him.

"…and you must do all of this alone. *Alone.*"

"But—"

"BUT NOTHING! You disgust me, *monkey!*" Christian yelled, and his shadow seemed to rustle, louder and louder, like a cloud of birds preparing to take flight.

Adam cowered back towards Jo.

Jo called out, raising their voice to be heard above the susurration of unseen wings. "Hey, at least tell me you'll make a truce with the thugs outside, so my shop isn't destroyed in your crossfire."

"I am the Crow King. I do not care what happens to this monkey-place. You can both bugger off for all I care." Christian's shadow became blacker and somehow more tangible, as if a giant crow were painted on the wall. Adam fell to the floor, sobbing.

"*Tabarnak,*" Jo muttered. "Okay, jackass. You want to play it this way? You're in my place, now… let's see how tough you really are." Jo grabbed a pair of stainless-steel bar needles from an open box on Scout's worktable, took two quick steps toward the wall, and jammed them into the Crow King's shadow—as if pinning it to the wall.

Christian screamed, a cocktail of pain, surprise, and fear. It shook the stained-glass window, and Jo was afraid it would shatter.

"*You bloody hussy!*" Christian roared as he convulsed.

Jo leaned on the needles as Christian wailed in agony. "Man, enough with the language. Keep swearing at me and I'll really make it *hurt.*"

Adam looked around, at the shadow crow pinned against the wall by Jo's needles, fluttering wildly, and how Christian was looking at Jo with something like pleading. Christian swallowed hard and licked his lips. "What do you want?" he hissed.

"I told you, dink. I can't make you take the kid under your roof, but honestly, this is probably the best thing you could do for him—shatter his illusions before it's too late. But you got us into this mess, and I won't have my studio destroyed by your dumbass macho rivalry. So you're going to go out there and make nice with Driftwood."

"And you'll let me go?"

"Yes."

"Fine."

"Promise me," Jo said, and their voice was dark.

"I promise," Christian muttered.

"Promise me," Jo repeated, and their voice was heavy as lead.

"I promise," Christian spat through gritted teeth.

"Promise me," Jo repeated a third time, and their voice was blacker than crow wings.

"I promise. I've sworn three times. Pull out the damn needles and let me be done with this cursed night."

Jo grabbed the needles and withdrew them with a twist. With a rush of wind, Christian's shadow was gone. And Christian with it. But Jo saw a large crow outside, near the high, open rear window. Jo would later tell Scout they swore the crow was clutching a huge leather jacket in its talons. Whatever the case, the jacket had disappeared from the store as fully as the Crow King.

Jo turned to the front window and saw Christian speaking to Shark Face. The big man wasn't happy, but despite some wild gesticulations, he took the jacket Christian held out to him and shrugged it on. He nodded once at Christian, then a bus drew in front of them blocking Jo's view. When it passed, Christian was gone again.

"All right," Christian called out from the back of the store.

"Lord, I will have a heart attack before this night is through," Jo muttered. "But before that I swear I'm gonna nail that damn window closed." Jo looked hard at Christian. "All right, what?"

"There is no war tonight between Driftwood Kryptic and the Queen Street Crows. Your little *den*," he spat the word, "is safe."

"And what about him?" Jo gave a meaningful look toward Adam.

"What about him?"

"What did you arrange about him, you pompous jackass?" Jo snarled.

"I had to offer Driftwood *some* form of compensation for their trouble, didn't I? I told them to take the price out of his hide. He's not a crow, so he's on his own. Driftwood Kryptic won't set a foot into your store or lay a finger on it," he smiled wickedly, "but they do seem ready to wait all night for the monkey to emerge. But don't worry, it won't matter to the crows," he laughed.

"Get the hell out of my space," Jo fumed.

"As you say," and Jo saw his shape and shadow blur with their own eyes. A huge crow flew up and out from the place where Christian had been standing.

"*Mon esti de tabarnak!*" Jo muttered, using Scout's favourite curse. "Definitely nail that bloody thing shut." Jo sat down heavily in Scout's chair and let out a world-weary sigh. But they knew the night wasn't over by a long shot yet. Jo swore to themself for a good long minute before finally regarding Adam. He was sitting on the floor, looking so much like a scared, homeless ten-year-old boy, Jo's heart almost broke.

"What... what was that!?" Adam half-spoke.

"Which part?" Jo asked.

"Christian... that crow... his shadow... your needles..."

"More things in heaven and earth, Horatio."

"Huh?" Adam said.

"Never mind," Jo said. "What it means is that the world is a big place. Full of all sorts of people and stories. And some things you wouldn't believe even if you saw them with your own eyes."

"And you're just okay with this?" Adam's voice trembled.

"I see my role as helping folks navigate some of the strange. But enough about me. What about you?" Jo asked.

"What about me?" he replied.

"Do you have any other place you can stay tonight?"

"Not really," his voice cracked, and Jo could see he was struggling to find his streetwise mask again.

"Okay, first things first. We need to get you away from here and keep you unsquished in the process. Right?"

"Yes, I guess." Adam was trembling.

"I've got an idea," Jo said and tried to smile reassuringly. Jo stood and patted Scout's chair. "Come on, sit here."

With some reluctance, Adam took Jo's spot and Jo studied him critically. "Wow. I normally refuse to ink someone as young as you… you're still growing and that can mess up the mojo. But tonight, I think we can take the risk."

"Ink? What… what do you mean?" He glanced at the Celtic rune pattern circling Jo's left bicep and the triad lightning bolt on their right arm.

"I mean a tattoo, kiddo. The Driftwood bullies still think of you as a baby crow. But we know you're not a crow at all. So if I can find your true essence and paint it on you, it should mask you from them. Although I guess it's more like pulling off a mask, but either way they won't know you."

"Do you think they are that dumb?"

Jo paused. "Kinda," and they both laughed a little, which helped. "But this is pretty powerful stuff, and this is where I do my best work."

Adam settled more easily into the chair.

"First, I need to explain that this is potent art. It will change you, and ultimately it will cost us both something."

"What do you mean? I have to pay you?"

"No, but… there's always a price to be paid for messing with the fabric of the world. I can't say what or when you'll have to pay, but you need to be aware."

Adam nodded solemnly. "What do we do?"

Jo crossed the room to their worktable and gathered up some ink, a tattoo machine from the sterilizer, and a new package of needles. They also grabbed the Bluetooth speaker. "First," Jo said unlocking their phone, "you find some music. Close your eyes and hit shuffle."

"Why?" Adam asked suspiciously.

"Well, two reasons. One, I can't work without music. And two, it will start giving me a road map to what to paint."

"You said that before, paint. Will it be temporary?"

"My bad. No, sorry, hun, this will be a real tattoo. And it will hurt. 'Paint' is just a term we use, like the body is our canvas." Adam closed his eyes tight and reached out to touch Jo's phone. Sting's *Shape of My Heart* came on and filled the studio with gentle guitar chords.

"I can work with this," Jo said.

Adam opened his eyes. "Does this mean you're giving me a tattoo of a heart?"

"No, the music channels the moment." Off his blank look, Jo elaborated. "It gives me ideas, but more like feelings than a specific image. Okay?"

"I guess."

"Trust me. However, I do need you to take off your shirt."

"Why?"

"Jeez, you ask a lot of questions! I'll be drawing over your heart. It's a powerful node on the body, and we need as much luck as we can get."

Adam slowly pulled his grimy tee-shirt off, and Jo was struck by how skinny and pale his chest was. Jo grabbed a bottle of rubbing alcohol and a cotton pad. As Sting sang about the "*sacred geometry of chance,*" Jo soaked the cotton and wiped down Adam's chest.

Jo inserted one of the bigger outline needles into the machine and started tracing a pattern on Adam's skin. Jo kept the pattern tiny, not wanting to prolong Adam's discomfort, and well aware that as he grew up, the image could distort grotesquely if they weren't careful. Still, the images in Jo's head were intricate and couldn't be rushed.

Despite the pain of the needle, Adam never winced or cried out, and Jo suspected he had been hurt far worse. Two hours, perhaps two dozen songs later, Jo sat back, satisfied. "I think we're good."

Adam craned his neck and tried to see what Jo had drawn. He couldn't quite make it out, so Jo picked up a mirror and showed him. Over Adam's heart was a small scene: a beautiful, dashing mouse standing on its hind legs and clutching a large thorn in its front paws. Behind it was a large lion's paw.

"What is this?" Adam's voice was awed at Jo's ability.

"Well, as we said, you're no crow. And I hate to disappoint, but in your heart of hearts, you're no bird at all. Still, I think we've found something better. Do you remember the story of the mouse who helps the lion by removing the thorn from its paw?"

Adam nodded, still staring at the image in the mirror.

"That mouse, while small, proved capable of moving mountains. So to speak. It showed courage, integrity, and cleverness. All good traits, kiddo."

"What does it mean for me?"

"Nothing, it's a picture." Adam looked crestfallen. "And also, everything. This is the shape of your heart, right now at least. I can't say what the future will hold, but I'm happy to help you as I can. And be your friend."

"I… I'd like that," Adam said.

"Now, a friend of mine works with kids who have no place to call their own. He's a good guy. Can I call him and see if he can help us sort out what's next for you?"

"I… I guess."

Jo nodded. "I understand. We'll take it slow."

Jo grabbed their cell and scrolled to find Davidson.

He picked up on the second ring. "Jo, what's going on?"

"Davidson, hey, sorry to call so late," but Jo knew Davidson was used to dealing with crises at all hours, and never seemed to sleep.

"Hit me."

"I've got a bit of a situation here. A kid with a good heart who needs a roof."

"You want to bring him over here?" Davidson asked when Jo finished filling him in.

"Would that be a problem?"

"Never, Jo. Come on over."

Jo bandaged Adam's chest and grabbed him a True Ink tee-shirt from the back room. He was so slight that even the smallest was a bit long, but at least it was clean. Jo handed Adam a sweatshirt to wear over top, and asked, "You ready to face the world?"

"Um…" Adam hesitated, once again seeming like a little kid and not the punk Jo had met hours earlier.

"I'll be with you every step of the way."

Jo slung their own jacket on, and the two walked out into the dawn light.

Shark Face blinked sleepily at them as they stepped out of the store into the chill morning. Adam involuntarily stepped closer to Jo, but Jo gave him a reassuring squeeze on the arm then turned to lock the door.

At the entrance to the alley, White Fang was on lookout. White Fang's head bobbed back and forth, as if trying to catch a scent. When Shark Face looked at him, he sniffed once, and growled, "Mouses."

Shark Face nodded and settled back against his bike, thinking they'd wait a little bit longer. The baby crow had to come out sometime.

Jo took Adam's hand in theirs and they walked down the street into the new day.

The Time-Stretcher

Kathryn Riley

By Emily's estimate, the asshat across the hall owed her two hours. And counting.

It had all started one evening a year ago. She was minding her own business, comfortably ensconced on her sofa in sweatpants and a faded University of Georgia tee-shirt, watching a House Hunters International marathon, wondering idly if her salary as a paralegal would ever finance a move from Atlanta to Wiesbaden or Mexico City or Pordenone. Maybe someday. She paused the show and was topping off her wine in the kitchen when she heard a faint thump and shuffle outside her apartment door.

It was a safe building—gated garage entry, security desk in the lobby, key fob, and all that. A single woman couldn't be too careful, as far as she was concerned. Rather than just opening the door to investigate, she took a second to look through her peephole.

Through the fisheye lens, she made out the face of the dour, middle-aged man who lived across the hall. She rarely encountered him or his short, disheveled wife, which was fine with her. She'd passed them in the hallway a few times; they seemed slightly antisocial. Not a problem. At least they weren't nosy, like the older woman two doors down who asked her, the first time they rode the elevator together, whether she was married and where she "churched."

The man—she had privately nicknamed him "Grumpy" and his distaff half, "Frumpy"—was bent over her doormat. This intrigued her, since the only thing on her doormat was her trash bin, ready to be emptied by the nightly trash valet service. Another perk of the high-rent district.

Somewhat mystified, she opened her door a crack. "Can I help you with something?"

Grumpy, dressed in a gray tee-shirt and red plaid pyjama bottoms, was setting a bag of trash on top of her bin. He looked up, obviously startled, and smiled sheepishly at being caught. "Oh, I just thought since your trash was already in the hall, you wouldn't mind if I added ours on top of yours." He unfolded to his full height, displaying a sallow complexion under a head of tousled, graying hair, and backed away toward his own front door.

Emily blinked, not sure how to respond. "Don't you have your own trash bin?"

"Yeah, but yours was already out there, so I didn't think you'd mind."

Emily took a breath. Stay calm, she thought to herself. "Well, I think it would be better if you used your own bin."

Grumpy continued backing toward his doorway. Narrowed his eyes and raised his voice slightly. "Oh, I need to use my own bin? Why is that?"

Emily felt a slightly Alice-in-Wonderland vibe developing. How had she ended up on the defensive here? She took another breath, blinked, struggled to stay firm but rational. "Because . . . we each have our own bin." Glancing behind him, she saw Frumpy open the couple's front door, no doubt to investigate their increasingly loud voices. Emily stared at her for a moment, then quietly retreated inside, closed her own door, and looked through her peephole.

Grumpy remained in his doorway, still facing Emily's apartment, with Frumpy standing slightly behind him. Emily heard his voice: "Boy, what a bitch. She's a real bitch."

Emily opened her door again. "Bitch!" he barked at her. She watched as Frumpy grabbed his arm and pulled him back into their apartment. Then he slammed the door.

Shaking now, Emily closed her own door again and double-checked the deadbolt. She stared through the peephole for a while, but the hallway remained quiet until the valet service rolled by with their huge cart around nine thirty. She opened her door a crack, quickly snaked her arm out to pull in her empty bin, and locked up again.

———

NOW, a year later, the incident had cost her every day. Her complaint to the manager had earned Grumpy a stern talking-to, but that was all. Emily no longer walked casually out her front door when she left to go to work or run an errand or use the fitness centre. No, first she tiptoed up to her peephole to make sure Grumpy wasn't in the hallway. On the rare occasion that he was, Emily waited silently until he was gone before she opened her own door.

She figured she spent an average of twenty seconds a day positioning herself behind her peephole and checking that the coast was clear. Over the course of a year, that was 7,300 seconds, or 121 minutes. Over two hours!

He owed her, she thought to herself as she finished her girl dinner (meatless Monday so half a baguette, a wedge of Brie, some sugar-free raspberry jam, and three cornichons). She took her empty plate to the kitchen and poured herself a glass of wine, preparing to settle in for an episode or two of Extraordinary Attorney Woo. If only there were some way she could make him pay back her lost time.

"I agree," a faint voice piped up from her living room.

She nearly knocked over her wine as she scuttled out of the kitchen and looked for the source. The TV? Siri?

As her eyes flicked around the room, they landed on a small, gnome-like figure standing next to the sofa: a tiny man, wearing a loden-green Alpine hat, sturdy brown shoes, a white pleated shirt, and—were those lederhosen? Her thoughts went wildly to a cuckoo clock her Aunt Karen had brought back from a Viking cruise through the Black Forest region.

Her mouth started to form the words "What the . . .?" but nothing came out. Instead, she opened and closed her lips a few times, in a perfect imitation of a cartoon fish.

She detected a faint German accent as the little man spoke. "Don't be alarmed. I'm just here to help you get your time back. The time that he owes you."

"Who are you? How did you get in here?"

He looked at her as if the answer were obvious. "I'm the Time-Stretcher, of course. You want to get back"—he paused to put on a tiny pair of spectacles and open a minuscule pocket watch that dangled from a chain around his neck—"two hours, right? I believe they're owed to you by"—here he paused again to consult a small notebook he pulled from his pocket—"and I quote, 'the asshat across the hall'?"

By now, Emily was interested enough to suspend her disbelief that there was a gnome in her living room. "That's right, just over two hours. What do you mean, I can get them back? How?"

He stared at her again as if she were an obtuse child. "Well, you have to agree to the Terms, of course." The word seemed to come out with a capital T, as if he were speaking in his native German.

"Okay . . . so what are these . . . Terms?"

"The Terms of our Agreement."

"So . . . maybe you could go over those with me?"

He sighed and hoisted himself up on the sofa, displaying knobby knees above his thick white socks. "You don't mind if I sit down for this, do you?"

Emily took a seat at the other end of the sofa and waited for him to continue.

"First of all, you have to understand that what you'll be getting is future time, not past time. In other words, you can't get back time that you've already spent. But I can stretch some of your future time so that it lasts a little longer."

"So . . . I'll be getting extra time in the future, to make up for the time I wasted at the peephole, is that the idea?"

"Now you're catching on."

"Well, that seems like a pretty good deal. Would I get the whole two hours at once, or how does it work?"

"Not quite. For a Level 1 infringement like this, you'll get back the time in five-second intervals."

"Oh. That hardly seems noticeable, but I guess it's better than nothing."

The Time-Stretcher looked slightly offended. "Believe me, there are times—no pun intended—when five seconds can seem like an eternity. And you might get several consecutive five-second intervals in one session."

"So . . . I might get, say, thirty seconds all at once, instead of just five seconds, is that what you mean?"

"Correct. The minimum time-stretch will be five seconds, while the maximum will be the total amount of time you're still owed at any given point. Right now, you're owed 7,300 seconds."

"Okay . . . but how much does it cost?"

The Time-Stretcher shook his head and laughed gently. "No cost to you. The time will go against Grumpy's account, since the triggering incident was an infringement on his part."

She wondered fleetingly how he knew her nickname for the asshat but brushed the thought aside. "Do I get to decide when I get the time-stretch?"

"No, part of the Agreement is that you'll have no control over that. But I can guarantee you that it will come while you're doing something you enjoy."

She smiled. "So not while I'm at the dentist or in a staff meeting, right?"

The Time-Stretcher smiled back. "No, definitely only when you're doing something you enjoy."

They both sat silently for a moment while Emily thought over the Terms of the Agreement he had outlined. She would get her wasted two hours back, in intervals of five seconds or more. She wouldn't have control over when the intervals came or whether they were strung together, but they would come only when she was doing something enjoyable. She couldn't see any downside.

"That all sounds fine to me. Do I have to sign something?"

"Not exactly. Just hold my watch while I seal the Agreement, and that'll make it official."

He scooched down the sofa until he sat next to her, so that she could reach out and put her hand around the tiny stopwatch around his neck. She caught a faint whiff of pine.

"Fir," he said, as if reading her mind. "A traditional symbol of time." He placed his hand over hers so that they both held the watch. He closed his eyes and proceeded to incant:

> *Let time be stretched so to repay*
> *The time that Grumpy stole away.*
> *Five seconds to Emily, at a time,*
> *Till Grumpy atones for his little crime.*
> *Let time be stretched only in pleasure,*
> *Make every moment one she'll treasure.*
> *We count 7,300 seconds*
> *As the total that we reckon.*
> *No more, no less, do I decree.*
> *As I say now, so mote it be.*

They both opened their eyes, and the Time-Stretcher climbed down from the sofa. "Well, that takes care of the Agreement. Everything's official now, so I'll be going." He trundled toward the balcony door. "I'll just leave the way I came in."

"Wait," she called. The Time-Stretcher turned back toward her with an exasperated sigh.

He raised an eyebrow. "Yes?"

"How will I know if I'm in my bonus time, or just in normal time?"

The Time-Stretcher gave her a slow smile. "Oh, don't worry, you'll know. That I can promise you."

By the time Emily got over to the balcony, he was gone. Apparently, a three-storey drop was not a problem for him.

She shook her head slowly and stared into the night, still slightly dazed. She went back to the kitchen, retrieved her wine, and took a deep gulp.

———

EMILY WOKE at seven the next morning after a restless night—after all, how often were you visited by a gnome? She started feeling a little more normal after coffee and a hot shower. Finally dressed for work, she left her apartment (after a peephole check, of course) and made her way to Beatrice, her sporty red secondhand Beemer. She started the engine, looked around at the beautiful fall day, and decided to put Beatrice's top down. It might be one of the last days warm enough for a convertible. Unusually for a Tuesday morning, her GPS showed no slowdowns on her route to work. She headed for the freeway, settling comfortably in the middle lane and keeping her speed at 65 mph, fast enough to feel the wind whipping her hair but slow enough to catch the occasional glimpse of other drivers viewing her with admiration or envy.

Four miles later, approaching her exit, she moved into the right lane and tapped the brakes—but nothing happened. She panicked, then made a split-second decision to stay on the freeway, fearing she wouldn't be able to slow down enough to navigate the U-shaped exit ramp.

She noticed, during all this, that she was enclosed in a kind of golden bubble, accompanied by a slightly warm sensation. At first, she thought it was the sun, but it was much more intense than the morning rays that came through Beatrice's open convertible roof. She watched her exit go past in the rearview mirror, then tapped tentatively on the brake pedal again.

This time, it worked.

She glanced down at her GPS screen and saw with relief that it was rerouting. Suddenly she heard the Time-Stretcher's voice. Where was it coming from—her head? No, the radio. She gripped the steering wheel.

"Good morning, Emily. Franz here." (Franz? she thought. Were they on a first-name basis now?) "Sorry to startle you. I wanted to officially confirm that you just had your first time-stretch. You probably saw a little glow and felt some warmth lasting exactly five seconds."

Emily listened while trying to dodge the morning traffic around her. "That was scary!" she yelled. "My brakes didn't work! I thought I was gonna crash!"

She heard a slight chuckle. "Now, now, calm down. You didn't come to any harm, did you? And you got to enjoy a few extra moments of that wonderful ride in Beatrice. Our agreement is that it will always happen when you're doing something that you like. Notice you were having a nice drive down the freeway, enjoying the admiring glances you were getting."

Emily blushed. "Well, just try to keep it from happening during rush hour, okay?"

"Noted. Now, remember, your next time-stretch might be five seconds, or you might get several linked together. You might have a time-stretch of ten seconds, or twenty minutes, or an hour. You'll know when it starts, because you'll see the glow and feel the warmth. But you won't know when it's going to end until the glow and the warmth stop."

The radio returned to her usual classic rock station. She followed the GPS as it rerouted her on an unfamiliar path to her office. Finally pulling into the parking lot, she checked the dashboard clock—twenty minutes late. Great. She ran a brush through her hair, put the roof up on Beatrice, and dashed into the office.

Nakesha, the office manager, rolled her eyes as Emily rushed through the door. "The staff meeting started fifteen minutes ago! You'd better get in now. Mr. Naylor was asking about you."

Emily opened the conference room door and tried to sneak in unobtrusively. As luck would have it, though, the only empty chair was halfway down the conference table, just two seats away from Mr. Naylor, the senior partner. Could things get any worse?

"So glad you could join us, Emily." All eyes swivelled to her for a moment, picking up on Naylor's sarcasm. "As I was saying, we'll need you to help Ryan research the Cavanaugh Insurance case."

"Yes, sir," she responded meekly. She booted up her laptop and quickly found the case files while she caught up with the agenda. At least she'd be working with one of the more tolerable (and attractive) junior partners.

Forty minutes later, she was back at her desk. Caitlin, her best friend among the other paralegals, paused as she walked by. "Rough night?" she asked sympathetically.

"No . . . I was just running late this morning. A little car trouble." Not exactly a fib, she thought to herself. "Of course, it had to happen the morning of a staff meeting."

"Of course. You still up for Sherwood's tomorrow after work?" The Sherwood Grill had a "networking event" every Wednesday from 5:00 to 7:00 p.m., with half-price drinks and free appetizers. Supposedly a venue for area businesspeople to make professional contacts, it wasn't a bad place to make the occasional personal contact as well. And free food was never wrong.

Emily made it uneventfully through the rest of the day and evening. She took special care to set her alarm fifteen minutes early for Wednesday morning. No way she could be late again, not after the staff meeting debacle. She laid out her clothes for the next day, carefully planning an outfit that would take her from work to the bar.

Work on Wednesday went smoothly and she and Caitlin drove separately to Sherwood's afterward, arriving early enough to snag a table. As they settled in over their glasses of the house Merlot, Ryan and another attractive professional type walked up to their table. "Mind if we join you?" Ryan asked, pulling out the chair next to Emily. "This is Hank Barnett, from Jenkins and Patel," he said, naming a boutique law firm in the area. Hank took the chair next to Caitlin.

They chatted for a few minutes over their drinks, then noticed that the buffet was open. "Why don't you ladies go up and help yourselves to some appetizers?" offered Hank. "We'll hold the table until you get back."

"Emily, you go ahead," said Caitlin. "I'm not too hungry just yet." She and Emily had a longstanding agreement not to leave their drinks unattended in a bar.

Emily returned from the buffet with a ladylike assortment of finger food on a small plate—olives, a fried wonton, a few mini-meatballs on toothpicks, and a cheese straw. She took her seat at the table while Ryan and Hank went to the buffet. Caitlin leaned in toward her. "Not a bad way to spend a Wednesday evening, right? I think Ryan might be interested in you."

"Maybe so, but I'm not gonna mix business with pleasure. I learned that the hard way at my last job." Emily sipped her wine, a warm feeling starting to set in. Best to stick to one glass. She nibbled at the cheese straw. So crisp and flaky, made with sharp cheddar and a kick of paprika. Such a nice golden colour, almost like it was glowing . . .

EMILY BLINKED SLOWLY AS she heard Caitlin's agitated voice. "Jesus, Emily, what came over you?" They were still at the same table, but Ryan and Hank were now standing on the far side of the crowded room, talking to another group. Emily and Caitlin's table was littered with a dozen empty plates, each scattered with crumbs, smears of sauce, toothpicks, and crumpled napkins. "You haven't stopped eating for the last fifteen minutes. You must have had two dozen of those mini-meatballs, not to mention about a dozen wontons and cheese straws and God knows how many olives. And five chicken satay skewers. It was downright embarrassing. At one point, you were actually moaning."

Emily burped quietly and stared at the plates. "Sorry. I'm not sure what happened to me. Everything just tasted so good. I guess I was hungry from only having a salad for lunch."

"Well, I think we need to get out of here before they kick us out. The bartender's been giving us the stink eye. You made four trips to the buffet and only bought one glass of wine."

"Okay," she said. "At least let me pay for our drinks." They gathered up their things, then Emily paid their tab, adding a generous tip. As they made their way to the front door, she saw Ryan glance in her direction, then look quickly away.

She drove home with Beatrice's top down, hoping the wind would clear her head. But she was still in a daze as she walked into her apartment, dropped her tote bag, and kicked off her kitten heels. She got as far as the sofa and flopped down on her back, loosening her waistband and closing her eyes. She just wanted to sleep off the food coma.

And sleep she did. She dreamt of tapas and meatballs and fried wontons and chicken satay, then moved on to a dessert course replete with mini cheesecakes, pistachio macarons with raspberry filling, and mixed fruit tartlets. She was dressed in a Roman toga, lounging on a mountain of cushions. Ryan (also in a toga) sat on an ottoman next to her, looking at her adoringly, feeding her one dessert at a time and reverently wiping her mouth with a hot, moist, lemon-scented towel, just like the ones they give you in business class on the airlines. Not that she'd ever flown business class, but she'd seen it in a Hallmark movie. He had just fed her a forkful of tiramisu when the faint sound of her phone ringing woke her up. Where was it?

Emily made her way to a sitting position on the sofa. Blinked at the sun coming through the balcony door. Glanced at the clock on the microwave: 9:30 a.m. Stumbled over to her tote bag and dug out her phone. It had stopped ringing, but a screen notification told her that she had a voicemail from Ryan's number at the office. Great.

Plopping back down on the sofa, she buried her head in her hands, too overwhelmed to panic. "Okay, Frodo, or Franz, or Time-Boy, or whatever the hell your name is, this has gotta stop."

She caught the faint scent of fir and opened her eyes. The Time-Stretcher sat at the other end of the sofa.

"You were sleeping so soundly and having such a nice dream, I decided to stretch it an extra hour and a half." He smiled, as if awaiting her thanks.

"Well, that was a genius move! Now I'm late for work again. If I still have a job, that is."

"Did you not enjoy the food?" he asked innocently.

"Do you mean the appetizers that I so charmingly hogged down at Sherwood's in front of my best friend from work and a good-looking junior partner? Or the fantasy food in the dream that made me oversleep?"

"Well, you must admit, I held up my end of the Agreement. Your time got stretched only during activities that were really bringing you pleasure."

"Yes, but you also embarrassed my friend, grossed out one of the junior partners, and now you've made me late for work and probably gotten me fired. How much longer will this last?"

"Well, let's see how much time you've stretched so far." Reaching into his breast pocket, he pulled out the tiniest Texas Instruments calculator she had ever seen and punched some buttons. "So far, you've stretched an hour and fifty minutes, so you've got ten minutes left."

Ten minutes. If she could make it through that, maybe her life would get back to normal. "Let me check this voicemail and find out how bad the damage is." She hit play and heard Ryan's voice:

"Hey Emily, I covered for you this morning with Naylor, told him you had to stop by Cavanaugh Insurance and pick up some files before you came in, but you need to get in here ASAP. Let me know when you get this."

She breathed a sigh of relief and texted a reply: "Thx for the save. Be there soon." She turned her focus back to the Time-Stretcher. "Look, I'm a paralegal, so I know something about contracts. How about if we add a codicil to the Agreement?"

"I'm listening," the Time-Stretcher replied in a cautious tone.

"I've got ten minutes left to stretch. Let me use them as I want, when I want."

He pursed his tiny lips. "Since you understand contracts, you know that I need what's called 'consideration.' What do I get for giving you control over your balance of ten minutes?"

Emily thought for a moment. "Look, I'll settle for one minute, and you can keep the unused nine. Further, I'll relinquish all rights to any future time-stretching to which I might be entitled."

"Okay, it's a deal. You know the drill." He scooched down the sofa to sit next to her, and together they grasped the tiny watch hanging from his neck as he chanted:

> *I hereby add this codicil*
> *To satisfy Emily's own free will.*
> *One minute of stretched time shall be*
> *The amount on which we now agree.*
> *She'll control the place to use*

The minute she stretches, and she'll choose
The minute that she will expand.
I leave that minute in Emily's hands.
And in return, to me she deeds
Her other nine minutes, and concedes
Stretched time in perpetuity.
As I say now, so mote it be.

MIRACULOUSLY, Emily made it to work by 10:30 that morning and managed to dodge the gimlet eye of Mr. Naylor for the rest of the day. Once home, she changed into a sweatshirt and elastic-waist joggers and ate a salad for dinner. At 8:00 p.m., she pulled a counter stool over to her front door and sat perched at a height where she could see through her peephole into the hallway.

At 8:05, Grumpy opened his door to put his trash bin out. Emily opened her own door, stepped out with her bin, and stood next to it in the hallway. She stared steadily at Grumpy as a warm, golden glow settled over her.

Grumpy later reported to Frumpy that Emily had locked eyes with him for what seemed like an eternity. "It was like she put some kind of spell on me where I couldn't move or talk. It kind of freaked me out, to tell you the truth."

Just to be on the safe side, he never left his apartment again without first checking his peephole—to make sure Emily wasn't in the hallway.

A Sacred Oath

Andrew Dunlop

"Fifty minutes or it's free, kid." It was Sal, slouched behind the counter of the pizzeria's reception area, who had growled it out. "It ain't just a business fad, it's a holy oath. Nobody's gonna wanna pay for cold pizza, and people order when they're hungry. You gotta get 'em their pies."

The words had impressed me when I was sixteen years old. In that halcyon youth, I had taken the gravitas that Sal had put into them to heart; Wizard Pizzas had been my first job, and to my young frame of mind, it was imperative that I uphold its good name.

In the years that had followed, I had found other work —gone to school, come back, joined in a half-dozen start-ups that had failed to ignite—and consistently found my way back to Sal and the pizzeria. The pizza hadn't been good in the nineties, and the decor had been outdated a decade before that. Still, the place had, if not thrived, managed to continue to limp along, despite not having updated the prices on a slice or a pizza since the decor had last been updated. People came in, partly because the pizza was cheap and partly on dares and bets. If the pizza quality factored into their decision-making, it was not a mark in the 'pro' column.

Sal himself seemed both ageless and very old, all at once, but he hadn't physically changed since I'd known him. He had been employee of the month back in the eighties, and his photo on the wall hadn't significantly changed since, saving the decade or so that he had flirted with a toupee. His hairnet had never provided him much service, and his beard net was stuffed to overflowing.

The perpetually smouldering cigar, dwelling between thin lips that never approached a smile closer than the demilitarized zone of a smirk, was probably the source of the yellow stains on his fingers that no amount of washing ever seemed to shift. It was the only pizzeria I'd ever heard of where staff actively avoided using their staff discounts. Sal said that the cigar ash was a proprietary secret of the sauce's flavour, and, in all honesty, he probably wasn't wrong.

Still, rathole fire trap or no, the place was an institution in our little town. Nobody was quite sure when it had been renamed to 'Wizard Pizza' but faded images of a cartoon wizard character wearing a purple pointy hat and with stars and moons on his robe suggested a failed attempt at branding that was best relegated to the dustbins of history.

But despite all of this—*all* of this—it was unaccountably a pretty good job. Sal might never have raised the cost of the pizza, but he paid well above the minimum tipping wage, and that more or less made up for the fact that the majority of the customers were ill-inclined to tip. If they were the sort to throw money around, they likely wouldn't have been ordering from a pizzeria whose health inspection certificates were suspect at best.

Nevertheless, of all the jobs that I'd had over my life at the point where things changed for me, it was the one that had the most stories. Some of them were funny—Sal's pizzas providing traction for a car stuck in a snow drift—and some were funny only in hindsight, like the surprising number of inveterate nudists that the town had who declined to throw on a robe before answering their front doors.

Holy oath? Well, my faith was tested from time to time.

It was a Podunk little town that I could just about spit across, and while the pies weren't good, the pizzeria was more than capable of churning them out *quickly*, so fifty minutes wasn't especially ambitious. The size of the town helped to contribute to Sal's financial success, such as it was; there really wasn't room in it for one pizzeria, much less two, which had kept it off of the map of more successful pizza chains for decades.

By far our oddest customer lived the furthest away, on a small farm right on the outskirts of the town limits and the delivery radius; he ordered a half-dozen pies with a frankly disgusting array of toppings. Pineapple? I wasn't a hater. Anchovies? Okay, on occasion. Head cheese? I didn't even know why we had head cheese as an option. And those were only three of the dozen or so toppings on the pies that, taken in concert, probably constituted a small war crime.

Still, the old guy that lived out there paid promptly and in cash, and was one of the few tipping customers that I had. The order was regular, and Sal usually had it prepared even before the call came in. The farm had ordered the same pizzas for almost forty years, at the same time, to the dot.

I never saw any other vehicles outside the old brick farmhouse when I came up with the pies, which suggested that not only did the scarecrow-like resident have weird taste, but he ate all six pies all by himself.

Better him than me.

Still, joining Sal in the 'aging surprisingly gracefully' club, the old fart hadn't visibly aged since I'd started on the route. I was forced to assume that due to some kind of misspent youth, he had become prematurely grizzled, and that this had somehow insulated him from any further grizzling as time walked forth upon its solemn business.

It was mid-August and scorching when I was on the run out to the farmhouse, a half-dozen war crimes on stuffed crust in the back and Mickey by my side. Mickey was my best friend coming up, and like many in the small town, had gravitated back to it, despite a lack of any real connections there. Mickey's family had, piecemeal, moved off to somewhere relevant, and as far as I could tell, they stuck around because they had a reputation as a capable handyperson and didn't want to chance moving out into the bigger world with hypothetical competition.

"I swear, we'll get outta this town someday." Mickey was riding shotgun because their truck had broken down and there was nothing better to do on a Friday night. I'd like to imagine that this constituted an endorsement of myself as a conversationalist, but I couldn't shake the undeniable truth that it probably counted more toward the dreariness of the burg.

"You've said that for years. So have I. We've both shot our shots and we're both pushing forty."

Mickey popped the lid off a tube of generic brand stacked chips and tossed one into their mouth. "So? When Mozart was our age, he'd been dead for two years. Everyone moves at their own pace. It's a scary world out there, and it's just not ready for us."

It was hard to argue with logic like that. I wanted to, though.

"Anyway, where would we go? What would we do?" I wasn't delivering pizza for my health, after all. "The economy's lousy, you studied film criticism, and I have a philosophy degree. The broader world is not falling over itself to give us jobs better than the ones we have now, and at least rent's cheap in town."

Mickey made a noise that was reminiscent of an irritated goose, but having been brought up with manners, declined to speak until their mouth was cleared of the offending chip. A scant moment later, they coughed and turned their head slightly. "Lack of ambition is the curse of the working class."

I tried to keep my eyes on the road, but the temptation to turn to face them was sublimated into a quirk of my head. "Who said that?"

Mickey's voice was deadpan. "I did, just now."

That was enough to snap my attention away from what I was doing at what proved to be a critical moment. "No, you goon, I mean who said that original—"

It might have been a suicidal porcupine, it might have been a pothole. It was, I was later to discover, something far more sinister than both. But there was an enormous blast of noise as the front driver's side tire burst like a balloon at a darts convention, and I fought to keep the wheel steady as navigation went from easy to difficult to impossible in a matter of seconds. My beat-up junker of a car skidded slightly but came to a stop.

We were both wearing seatbelts, and the air bags in my car hadn't worked for longer than I'd owned it, but we were both shook up and not a little sore. I took a moment to catch my breath.

"The *hell* was that."

Mickey was annoying sometimes, but a solid head in a crisis. "Tire blowout. You've got a spare and a jack? I can help change it."

"I wouldn't drive anywhere without them in this town." There was a garage in the town, but like so many other small businesses, it had withered on the vine as the staff and equipment had aged. All of this together meant that if I'd had to call for a tow truck, I would probably be there until dawn unless old Gus had remembered to charge the batteries on his hearing aid and had a fighting chance of hearing the phone.

Mickey popped the trunk and, digging through the various junk that resided within, produced the spare and a jack. "I'm happy to change the tire but it might take a little time. I'm pretty sure this spare has whiskers on it."

I sighed. "Not much choice, is there?"

I was painfully aware of time ticking away as Mickey laid out the tools, got the car on the jack, and put the new tire in place. Maybe I didn't believe that 'fifty minutes or it's free' was a holy oath, but I had been brought up with an unhealthy sense of responsibility, and I was a professional. I'd agreed to deliver the pizza in a timely manner—to one of the few guys on my route that tipped—and now it was going to be late.

Rationally, it was bound to happen sooner or later. It

just felt bad that I was going to be late delivering these pies to someone who had been ordering them for so long, and quite possibly never ate anything else. Even if I could maneuver six pizzas to a position where I could carry them while running, the farm house was still ten minutes away by car.

All told, Mickey did a surprisingly fast job of replacing the tire—they really *were* good at working with their hands —but it would take at least ten minutes to get to the farm-house even if I sped, and the spare wasn't built for highway speeds.

I got back in the car, feeling a bit rotten. It would be one thing to screw up anywhere else, but... Wizard Pizza had been my home away from home for years, depressing a thought as that might be. I might not believe that 'fifty minutes or it's free' was even much of a promotional stunt, but in addition to not getting paid for the pies, it always felt personal when I felt like I was letting Sal down.

I went as fast as I could... as fast as it was safe to go. If everything had gone exactly perfectly, we might have still been there on time, as unlikely as that seemed. But it was a comedy of errors: here, a group of ducks crossing the road; there, a stalled vehicle. All told, we made it only three minutes late; or, put another way, we were three minutes past the essential cut-off time.

The farmhouse did not loom because it was incapable of looming; sitting low and miserable upon the land, it slouched before me when I pulled up. More concerning, it seemed to be shrouded in a haze of low-lying fog that was atypical for the area and time of year, and as I walked up to the door, carefully balancing the generic white cardboard boxes that held the pizzas, I felt a sudden apprehension that I had difficulty putting into words.

The old guy that lived within emerged, fanning away vapour that twisted and trailed around him with a broad-brimmed hat, coughing and hacking. He growled when he saw me.

"You're late, damn you." A breath. "Damn us all, I suppose."

There was a sliver of trepidation in his voice, yet I didn't think that he was afraid of me. Which demanded the question: what *was* he nervous about?

"Yeah man, we caught a flat as we were driving down here." I gestured to the car by way of evidence; the spare was smaller than the other tires and didn't match. "Sorry, I know we should have called, but this whole area is a dead cell zone." I made the mistake of trying to show the bright side of the situation. "But hey, good news—we do stand by our motto of fifty minutes or it's free—you get some free pies out of the deal."

The words electrified him, his face contorting into a rictus of rage. "No, you fool!" This was never a pleasant thing to call someone, and reminiscent of no small number of Disney villains dialogue-wise. "It's free. *It's* free. This was no paltry promotional promise! By your tardiness, you have doomed the tri-county area! Perhaps the world!"

I can only imagine that my face was a study in confusion, and while not exactly flattering, my tone of voice was consistent with the findings of that study. "Uh, what?"

"You may as well come inside," the old man growled. "Bring your friend, too. If we're all going to die, you might as well die somewhat less the gormless idiots that you both are." After a moment's pause. "Bring the pizzas."

You didn't often hear the word 'gormless' used these days, much less correctly.

Mickey hopped out of the car and I followed the old grouch into the house. It was weird, but despite his low-grade mutterings about the end of all things and general state of hygiene (best expressed in negative terms), I didn't feel much concern for my well-being. He didn't seem the type.

The inside of the farmhouse belied the rundown appearance of the outside, and the wizened and grubby appearance of its solitary resident. It was reasonably clean, if a bit dusty, but lacked the baked-in grime that seemed to follow the old guy around. It definitely lacked the smell that I had mentally associated with someone who lived on head cheese pizzas.

"So what's all this about the end of the world?"

The old man grinned a crooked smile, walking into what seemed to be a nicely appointed office space that had apparently been designed sometime in the seventies. The walls were lined with leather-bound books, with one sitting open on the desk. The pages had gilded edges, and the book was written in a language that was not familiar to my eye, with strange and slightly disturbing pictures.

"I took possession of this place in 1969. There was an evil in these woods, something out of nightmares and smoke." He gestured about. "I was seeking to make a sanctum for myself and some other searchers of mystical truth, and so I set about to hunt *it*."

It sounded crazy. Still, I could believe the old man to be an occultist; the decor in the library, now that I looked around, was rather skull-candle-and-mirror forward.

"What, like a monster?" Mickey asked. It sounded crazy

said aloud, and yet he seized upon our moment of credu-lousness like a wolf to meat.

"Yes, precisely! An escapee from an ancient dungeon dimension, manifesting in the real world. My team and I hunted it out, with fire and steel and reason, but discovered too late that it had a small following of worshippers local to the town."

I believe that the words that sought to escape me had a lot in common with bovine manure at that point, but Mickey held up a hand. "No, wait, I heard about... well, something like this. A bunch of unexplained disappear-ances up to the early seventies, when they just kind of stopped. It's a cold case, and sort of a local cryptid. I was thinking about trying to make a movie about it for the film fest in the city."

I quelled the urge to call the old guy out, but it didn't leave my mind entirely. "Okay, so what happened then?"

The old guy scowled. "The cultists ambushed us. Most of my team was killed. We were forced to retreat back to the farmhouse, and night was falling. We needed to recover... we needed food. So we ordered in a pizza, and Sal brought it out. Just as he showed up, the monster attacked." In the shadowy room, I felt a shiver slip across my spine. "We were in no position to hold it off but Sal did something we didn't expect. He offered the monster the pizza he'd brought.

"It accepted it, and he led it by the pizza out to the back, where there was a well. He got it all excited for the pie and then tossed the pizza into the well, and it went in after it. My few surviving colleagues and I were able to create a mystic working across the top of the well, sealing it in, but with a condition. The pizza box had the promotion on it: 'fifty minutes or it's free!' and because we had built our bindings around its willingness to enter the well in search of the pizza, the dread pact was sealed.

"We had saved the town—the county—from a ravenous beast. But should the pizza ever take more than fifty minutes to arrive, *it* would be free. With the aid of my resources and mystical acumen, Sal has kept the pizzeria in business and has scarcely aged, lo these fifty years."

The story was absurd, but somehow it held together. It was silly, but silly in the way that gave it verisimilitude. The unintuitive solution that gets the job done; a monster might well be immune to every *sensible* method of dealing with it, making a nonsensible one the only one that could conceivably work. Of course, stupid solutions had consequences.

I eyed what I had thought to be the sculpture of a skull that the old man had on his desk. Now that was a loaded question I was entirely unwilling to ask. Happily, a backup question presented itself, and I leapt on the opportunity like a jaguar.

"So you don't actually eat the pizzas every week?"

The old man gave me a *look*. "Head cheese, pineapple, and anchovy on one pie? Times *six?* Thank you, no, I choose a life that allows me occasionally to see something other than the inside of the outhouse door." It was a hard point to argue against.

The outside windows were now fully obscured by the cloud. Mickey looked out nervously. "I don't know exactly what time sunset is supposed to be tonight, but I don't think it's yet." And it was dark, like night had fallen early.

The old man shook his head. "I do not know if I have the strength still to face the beast. I never did when I was fifty years younger, if it comes to it. Had Sal not been there..." The sentence dangled, tempting fate with an ominous 'what if' that might well yet be realized then and there. I swallowed hard.

Time to step up and see if there was more to me than there had been for the thirty-odd years that I'd been look-ing. Evidence suggested that there wasn't, but it was all circumstantial at best. "I guess Sal's right. It's a holy oath." Time to figure out what I actually believed.

Mickey grimaced. "You know I'm there for you, thick or thin." They very clearly didn't want to say the words, but the bonds of friendship proved stronger than self-preserva-tion in a moment that probably shocked both of us equally.

"No," I said, shocking myself further. "If it doesn't go right, you need to drive the geezer here to town." I rounded on the old man. "You... grab whatever you might need in order to stave the thing off. If it's going to hurt people in town, then they need to evacuate, or fend it off, or... something."

He looked a little taken aback but became a blur of motion, filling a large carpet bag with books and trinkets from the desk and shelves around the library. I headed to the back door.

I didn't owe the town anything. It had been a place where I'd grown up and couldn't get away from. But my failure to launch didn't reflect on the burg that was only one short generation away from fading from the map due to lack of giving-a-crap. But full of weirdos and losers like me as the town was, the people there genuinely didn't have what was coming, coming.

The world outside was dark as night—darker, without sun, or moon, or any of the thousand sources of light pollu-tion that you got even this far out in the sticks. My cell-

phone's flashlight beam made it maybe two inches in before
being swallowed whole by the ravenous darkness.

I held the pizzas in one arm. I stepped in.

There was no direction. Up and down are oriented by
gravity, and I could no more tell if something I held would
drop than fly away. Forward was the direction I was facing,
but without landmarks, I had no way of knowing if I had
turned or been turned. Still, I walked forward. I had the
inklings of a plan, but it involved not being noticed
too soo—

i am hungry

The words weren't spoken but I suddenly had memory
of hearing them, as real as my own thoughts, self, and the
world before I had entered the darkness.

this world was given that i might consume

That was unsettling. The darkness even swallowed up
the sound of the gravel of the back patch crunching under
my feet, but I had been up to this farm a few hundred
times; rain or shine, snow, sleet, or gloom of night... sometimes the post office had even had me carry up some
letters. I didn't make a habit of skulking around the prop-
erty, but I knew where what I was looking for was *supposed*
to be.

i have too long been denied

Those words came with a searing sense of timelessness.
This was a being that had no conventional sense of time,
but a burning impatience. I was understanding only a frac-
tion of what it was, being perceived from every angle at
once, as I strode through everything that made it up.

you waste your brief time

And yet, as alien as it was, it *wanted* things, things that I
could understand. It consumed... well, so did all living

things. It was complex, had needs it conveyed and ones it withheld. And for some reason, it really liked Sal's pizzas.

I opened my mouth to speak and choked on the blinding smog that encompassed me. I forced my way through—it was important, essential that I get the words out. "I will destroy the pizzas."

If it could have consumed me on the spot, it would have. I had no idea what it needed… if I needed to succumb to something or perhaps just die. Maybe the combination of anchovies, head cheese, and pineapple made something that approximated a human corpse in ways other than just smell. But it couldn't stop me, and that's why it was threatening me.

you cannot

It did not—could not—exclaim. Nevertheless, there was an urgency to these words that trespassed in my mind before. "I can. I will. And you will have no more unless you return to the well." Years of delivering pizzas had well-honed my knowledge of all the ways that a pizza could be utterly ruined, and years of customer service had reduced my empathy for customers to a hair below loathing.

the compact was broken

That was a start for negotiation. "We are willing to be generous in making good the lack. Call it an extra pie a week, moving forward."

"Or you can take your chances out in the world again. It's a scary place, and it doesn't like people that don't try to fit in. There may be a time to spread your wings but some-times surviving until you're ready is the best you can do." Those words stung my throat as I spoke them but they came from a true place. "Who knows? Maybe there will come a time when the world is ready for your particular kind of unmaking." Hope for the future, even thin hope, can make the unpalatable manageable. It worked for everyone else, after all.

addition: cheesy breadsticks

"Deal."

My foot hit the stone wall of the well and I pitched the pies into an abyss that wasn't significantly different from the one that had too recently surrounded me. There was the howl as of an abyssal wind, and the all-encompassing smoke sucked itself away, leaving me breathless as it stole the polluted air from my lungs.

I fell to all fours, threw up a little, blinking as the harsh light of twilight stung my eyes. And Mickey was there, and the old geezer, helping me, carrying me to the farmhouse. Colour was flowing back into the world with a sluggishness that made me wonder exactly how long I had taken to cross the yard, and if I'd suffered some brain damage in the process.

Once I could talk again, I made sure that the bread-sticks and the extra pie were added to the order.

IT'S NOT A GLAMOROUS JOB. I've seen altogether too many naked people, chiselling cheapskates, and pizzas whose very presence on a menu probably constitute biolog-ical warfare, or at least a crime against epicurean palates everywhere. I haven't left town yet, but maybe I will when the world and I are ready for one another.

But like it says on the box: fifty minutes or it's free. It's not just a business fad.

It's a holy oath.

Woman of Stone

R.P. Ferguson

They've hunted me for five days, and until now I've always slipped away unscathed, my great ailment being my lack of sleep. The days I've managed well enough. I watch for danger, careful of every step, resting only when hidden. But night after night of being wary of each little sound of the wild has positioned my thoughts so that I cannot rest. Weariness is a rot that brings weakness to every part of the body, and weakness most certainly brings about clumsiness.

My clumsy descent into this cavern that was to be my shelter for the night has likely turned it into my tomb. For I, who have been called strong and able, am now weary and wretched, and so what was to be my climb down from the narrow maw became instead a swift and brutal fall. I don't even remember the final impact, only the small collisions on the way down. Time was lost to me, and I cannot say when I emerged from throbbing oblivion into the stale darkness of this prickly, gravel-crusted floor to find all of me bruised and my left arm snapped beyond mending above the wrist.

If there was any light by which to see, I'm sure the arm

would be swollen and purple. More than anything I can feel my blood concentrated there. But in forgetful moments, I still attempt to turn my hand this way or that, and the resulting pain is the sharpest, most instant punishment I have ever known.

How can I be so aware of something one moment, and so forgetful the next? It is the height of stupidity. And that explains all of it. I lie upon the floor of this cave with a broken arm, gritting my teeth to hold myself back from wailing my agony to the uncaring dark because I have been stupid, because I have been careless. The time for berating myself must end now, though. It won't get me through this.

Turning on my side is miserable enough, but propping myself up and bracing and pushing against the rocky ground tests how long I can endure misery. Apparently, I can endure it long enough to stand, wobbly, and now it becomes a test of balance. Can I stand with feet planted on uneven ground while my head lolls and my vision whirls and swims drunkenly through the dark, top-heavy, poised to tip this way or that? It is simple, I tell myself. Stand. Stand still.

I can. I do. I find my balance. Now, carefully, slowly, I pull my wool shirt up over my head with my useful hand, and down and off, freeing both arms from the sleeves. It is cool in the cavern but not as cold as the night had been outside of it. The shirt's warmth had been a comfort, but it will serve me better as a sling. It takes me several attempts and much painful jostling to get it rightly tied and tight, but now, having the snapped arm upheld to my chest, I know I can travel, and more importantly, I seem to remember not to turn the hand.

The cavern is not fully dark, I learn. A vague and

shifting dimness, a hint of light outlines a curving wall of rock in the direction opposite of where I estimate I entered. I inch toward it, always taking care to note my forward foot is touching solid ground before I commit my weight to it. Nearing the curving wall, the travel becomes better. Strewn with fewer and fewer rocks, the floor becomes smooth, even soft with an occasional coating of fine sand, and that dim hint of light becomes more and more real to my eyes that yearn to see anything.

Rounding the bend I take on an almost normal pace, as I can now see most of my surroundings. This proves fortunate as I see the way is riddled with pointed, tube-like rocks reaching down from a low ceiling. Navigating any further without vision would have had me knocking my head against them again and again.

Although it has been quieter with softer ground underfoot, something like a breeze now tickles the edges of my ears from time to time, and with it a chill descends through me, crawling down along my skin from head to toe, bringing soothing coolness to my swollen arm. There is something almost rhythmic, or even syllabic, to the breeze. Mistaking it for a voice, I stop and listen, but it dies out and I am left in silence—except for a faint trickling of moisture —to scan the narrowing tunnel before me. Far less dim than it was when I set out, the space sparkles, subtly, its walls and rock formations, near and far, alive and aglow with speckles like gems, rubies, diamonds.

I would swear these jewel-encrusted rocks do make their own light, for I have no other explanation to why I am not in darkness, to why it is only brightening as I go. Moving forward, ducking down out of necessity, the breeze—the voice—returns to my ears, but I harden myself against wondering. I must get as far from where I entered the cavern as I can, lest my pursuers follow me down here. It won't serve me to stop and ponder. I have spent much time down here, and if I could find the maw in the craggy hill-side, so can they.

Ignoring the voice proves unreasonable, however, now that it—she—whispers words: "Welcome...You are most welcome. My domain welcomes you, traveller. My domain opens to you... My domain embraces you, traveller..."

Each syllable, though soft and quiet, is pronounced with great care and clarity and every word of it feels near to my ears, bringing back the chill, the soothing coolness that crawls over my skin.

"See the rocks that glimmer and wink," she says, from nowhere and from everywhere. "They watch you so that I may see you. As they brighten, you approach me. You draw nearer. You are right to let them guide you. My domain is open to you."

"What do you want of me?" I say to the rocks, to the empty, humid tunnel.

"I want you safe. I want you soothed. I want you restored."

I sense nothing beyond frankness in her tone, but how can I trust a woman who watches without eyes and speaks without a mouth? Still moving deeper into the tunnel, I reach a stretch where I must crawl, one-handed, under a crowded cluster of rock tubes like a grill or long-toothed comb. Further and further down they reach, and although they sparkle and are dazzling to behold, I don't like that I now must lie prone to fit beneath them. My weight pressing into my bad arm is agony I cannot endure, so I twist and turn about to lie on my back.

The best choice I have is to scoot like a worm, kicking my feet as one while digging the elbow of my good arm into the sandy ground to wrench me further along. It proves very slow going. As my head swims free of the long-reaching rock tubes at last, I am panting, thirsty for air in the way dogs are when they've overworked themselves in stupid pursuits. Rolling on my side and bracing against the ground, I rise slowly, and doing so, learn the tunnel has opened to a vast, suddenly high-ceilinged chamber.

After a short landing of sand, all the floor, all the walls, and seemingly all the ceiling, are sheer and smooth and seamless surfaces of rock and all of it is bright and gleaming, crowdedly bespeckled with every colour, every glow of every gem and every gleam of every noble metal, some of them still in their brightness, others pulsing across a spectrum of rhythms. I step forward, cautiously, and the multi-coloured radiance washes over me, painting my skin to make me a great herald of rainbows and festivities.

She speaks, and in so doing she emerges from the once seamless rock wall, a woman-shaped body that swells, protrudes, and now breaks free of the surface: "Traveller, you are here in my domain. I offer you my hospitality. Please, have a seat."

Abruptly, beside me, a mound of stone rises from the floor, grows, and assumes the shape of a four-legged, tall-backed chair.

Gracefully, the woman moves toward me at a regal, unhurried pace, and I sit upon the chair she summoned for me. I am too in awe not to. With an upturning of her palms and a wriggling of her fingers, the ground between her and I quakes. Startled, I shift in place, wanting to flee in fear, but I don't. I stay. I think I'd be more afraid to leave.

From the trembling floor sprouts a stone pillar of considerable thickness. Rising to half my height, it suddenly splays outward. At last it rests, having become a smooth table of stone with me perfectly seated at it. Reflecting the sparkling ceiling overhead, the table holds a pool of clear water at its centre.

Looking up from the stillness of that enticing pool, I see the woman has stopped to stand opposite me at the table. Her limbs and torso and face, free of any garments, are all perfect silver smoothness, glistening like polished metal, but everywhere gems sparkle upon her, the greatest of all being her eyes—one fiery topaz, the other bold emerald—equal in size, but startlingly separate in colour. Her lips part without any lines creasing upon her face—it is shockingly inhuman: "Drink."

And a stone goblet sprouts up from the table, taking shape above my lap. I regard the water, and now the woman.

Her topaz and emerald eyes do not blink. "The water, traveller, is the purest you will find in all the world. Deeply pure. From deeper underground than humankind could ever delve. Drink. Drink deeply. I can feel your thirst."

"Hell," I say as I grasp the goblet and, reaching forward, dunk it into the water at the table's centre. It is in fact the coolest, cleanest, most refreshing substance I have ever tasted. I guzzle the goblet to emptiness, refill it from the pool, and drink again.

The stone woman's lips have pressed into a resolute smile. She nods reassurance while I drink and compose myself. With that motion, a formation like hair sways upon her head. There are patterns, waves, even curls in that formation, intricately chiselled but without separation, all of it moving as one.

"Men follow you, traveller," she says with great somberness. "Four men. All this time I have felt them sneaking through my domain. They are very near now. Their intent murderous."

"So I have feared."

"Why do they seek you?"

"I bloodied the mouth of a soldier." I take another drink, and pause, considering my words. "The soldier, seemingly for no other reason than his own delight, harassed an old beggar... so I bloodied the soldier's face to make him stop... and in doing so, knocked him flat. What I didn't know, soon enough, was that soldier was the nephew of someone important. So, men were sent to capture me, beat me, flay me, to restore the pride of the soldier, his uncle, and now, I suppose, themselves."

The woman nods once, her stone face holding no discernible expression. "You cannot defend yourself from these men... as you are."

I snort laughter, looking down at the hand tied up in the tattered sling. "I'll try, but I'll bet you are right." I shake my head, a part of me disbelieving all that surrounds me. "So is that why you lured me to you, to hear of my grand misadventures?"

She takes a step forward, seeming to bend, or slant, toward me. "I have opened my domain to you to make you an offer. You may accept or deny this offer and the hospitality of my domain is still yours—while you live."

I scratch at my head of dusty hair. "The offer?"

"I restore the use of your hand, and I arm you so that you can defend yourself."

"And the cost of this restoration, this miracle?"

"You will serve my domain. You will belong to it."

I look about me, studying again the sheer, jewel-encrusted walls and ceiling. "I will belong to this chamber?"

"My domain is every space that yawns and sprawls open beneath all the world. Beneath mountains and valleys. Beneath, even, seas."

I stare into her topaz and emerald eyes, feeling lured, tempted beyond explanation. At last I shake my head, as though to break free of a trance. "I serve no man, or woman, or being. I am free, and so I shall remain."

"Free to die," she says with flat sombreness, and turns her back on me.

As she steps away, I hear scraping and shuffling behind me—the men, my pursuers, beginning to crawl free of the tunnel. Glancing over her immaculately smooth shoulder, she says, "The offer stands while you live. Should you submit to the offer, all you need do is submerge your hand in the water of this table, and my domain will make it mighty."

Rising from my stone seat, I reach out to her with words: "Where do you go?"

"To relinquish this form and rest. I must be absent for the coming violence. It would tempt me toward action. But I cannot spill the lifeblood of men."

"Cannot or will not?"

"Must not." And she steps to the sheer wall, pressing herself to it. And she becomes the wall, is absorbed into it.

"Alright here, good sirs, we have him," a voice growls at my back.

Turning, I recognize his ugly, haggard face, his slack,

cruel mouth that now twists into a satisfied sneer. He is so confident he has me that he's left his weapon sheathed.

Noticing that, I decide there is nothing else I need consider. And so, lunging, closing, I have my hand around his scraggly throat before the other three men have risen from the cave floor to join him. There is time, I find, to buckle his knees and bring him down flat to the cold ground, time to pin him with my weight as my grip tightens on his neck and his hands alternate smacking at my arm, clawing at my fingers, reaching for my eyes, his mouth a tight grimace that hasn't lost its look of surprise.

"Get off!" a voice rings out from the tunnel's opening, accompanied by grunts, heavy breathing, all of it echoing over itself in the close chamber, and before I can see it, a body, or bodies, shove me, tumble over me. I fall and roll. Reckless fists and feet have found me. My head, my back, my stomach. I kick and kick and twist, doing what I can to bar them back with one arm. Before me I see eyes lurching down, and kicking as hard as I can, I make good contact this time. That man falls with a howl.

Scooting back, I crawl under the stone table. Twisting, stumbling, I get my feet beneath me on the other side and stand, holding the table. My head is throbbing, and my nose throbs swollen and hot. Blood is in my mouth. I spit.

Two men stare me down with heavy, unhappy eyes. The man whom I throttled staggers behind them. The man whose face I kicked must still be on the floor. In unison they lunge from either side of the table. I swing my fist at one, but swing wide, and instantly the other has me by the waist, and now together they slam me sprawling onto the table. The ugly man I throttled has got his balance back, for he smiles down at me as the other two hold my feet and arm.

I twist. I growl.

He grips my head between his hands.

"I say, good sirs, that was quite a fuss, was it not?"

"Aye."

"Aye."

I hear the other men laugh gruffly as, abruptly, he slams my head into the table murderously. Overhead and all around me, the jewels of the chamber walls and ceiling all wink at once and smear together, and with that comes a sensation that the world is slanting, falling away underneath me.

He slams my head again, and now the only thing I'm sure I am perceiving is their cruel chorus of laughter and snorts, echoing, resounding. Somehow my searching, wriggling fingers find the puddle of water at the centre of the table. Experiencing that coolness, as when I had drunk that water, I feel a sudden vigour and clarity overtake me. The world steadies, and in that moment, surprising the men, I wrench suddenly to my side, plunging my hand into the water. It is deeper than it should be, as though I could submerge my entire self into it, as though the table somehow contains an entire world, a deep sea within the stone.

But I don't dive in. I withdraw my arm. Forgetting, for a moment, the men, I disbelieve the sight of my own hand. Glistening from the water, dripping, sparkling, it has become a solid fist of bejeweled stone. I know, with certainty, it is very heavy, but I feel a strength within me that tells me I can lift its weight as easily as always.

Overcoming their shock, the men bear down on me, tightening their grip with clawing fingers. Too strong to be restrained, I swing the stone club of my hand up and behind me, bashing the man who had slammed my head to the table. He crumples to the ground, and so I wrench myself in that direction and, rolling, fall from the table.

Dizzy and stumbling, I reach for the stone chair, and clambering, somehow prop myself up from it. I turn to find the two men who still stand have drawn long knives.

Suddenly the walls of the chamber speak: "The offer is accepted."

The men with their knives drawn look about them, searching fearfully for the source of the words.

From nowhere and everywhere, she speaks again: "Remember, I have not only restored your hand to strength, I have armed you."

I study the men before me. Though they still outnumber me as they always have, and though they have blades and I do not, they look suddenly completely unsure of their victory, of themselves. Deep within myself, now rising to the surface of my thoughts, I have only one wish at this moment: a blade of my own. If I could just have that, and no other thing, I could overcome them. I know it.

One of the men, looking very anxious, blinking continually, takes a trembling step toward me, as beside him his companion, reacting sluggishly, mimics him with a slight delay. They step again, converging and slicing at me.

But my hand has already met them. Swinging broadly, still longing for the blade I do not possess, I find my stone hand has elongated—all resemblance to the arm I used to call my own gone, both in flesh and in form—changed and lengthened into a thin, severe, lethal point. The end of my arm, now twice its length, is what can only be described as a sword of stone. Already it has cut and shattered the knife of one of the men and cut through and

severed the arm of the other. He falls to the floor screaming, a sound more shrill than I imagined he could
produce.

As I advance, the other man looks to him, looks back to
me, hesitating, but I don't hesitate. I swing the stone sword,
the long-tipped arm, until they are both on the floor, until
they are both motionless and quiet.

Behind me, beside me now, I feel—before I can see—
she has emerged, reassuming the woman shape. The stone
sword has become a stone hand again, fingers bound into a
tight and seamless fist. She takes it in her smooth, intricately
carved hands, raises it to her shining topaz and emerald
eyes.

"Traveller, my traveller. You are of me now. Of this
domain. I am so happy. You were so valourous. So brave
and mighty. Truly I am blessed this day. I am honoured."

"I… I didn't want this. Any of it. I…"

Her voice falls very quiet, very sombre: "But you
chose."

I snort. "What choice did I have?"

"The only one that I could give. It matters not. You are
of me."

"I won't be made to serve." I turn and push, forcefully,
to brush her aside, but I have forgotten entirely how strong
my arm now is. My stone hand has pushed straight through
her torso. In great shock, her seamless lips abruptly part
and her sheer, expressionless face now sways forward to
gape down at the crater I have unintentionally made in her.

"I… forgive me… I didn't…"

She says nothing as the sleek surface of her body breaks
into innumerable cracks, her face looking terribly sad,
staring unwaveringly at the powerful, monstrous hand she

gave to me, until she loses all shape and bursts, shattering into a rain of fragments that scatters all across the floor.

I survey the death and damage I have brought to the chamber, taking care to ensure none of the four men will ever hound my trail again. It disgusts me, what I've done, what I have become, but I know I never deserved the punishment they sought to give to me, and so I refused to wait for it, refused to accept it when it came. What free person would not do the same?

I kneel down at last and examine the broken pieces of the woman of stone. In my hand of flesh, I feel the cool smoothness of her fragmented shards, the impossible slickness of finely crushed jewels that once were of her body.

Softly, clearly, the walls speak, causing the small hairs of my nape to rise: "Take what you can carry, traveller. But know that not all that shines beneath the surface will remain luminous above it."

Crawling back through the tight tunnel and locating the rise of loose rocks down which I first tumbled when I entered the cavern proves to be hours of toil. I am enlivened, however, to discover, after focusing intently on my need, that I can turn my clublike hand back into loose fingers. Using both hands and keeping slow, careful to keep my thoughts focused on my need for escape, my need for freedom, I now climb up through the maw of the cave and feel the light of day upon my skin.

I spend my next days out on the surface, under blue skies or white clouds, and under stars at night. But time alone, time away and free from the cavern reveals a sombre truth to me: my stone hand has begun to stiffen, and in a dull way it aches. Getting it to do anything has gotten harder and harder. There is even a sensation that more and more of my arm, of me, is becoming stone, and with that I tend more and more toward sluggishness. Worst of all, the light of morning no longer warms me, for that sense of flat coolness beneath the surface never leaves.

I know I must get to a cave, a mine, some dark chasm, and descend below the world to replenish whatever is being depleted in me. But I also know that would mean reentering her domain. Is freedom ever to be found in servitude?

Hell, I must make sure to survive first. I can ask myself that question later.

We Don't Do That Kind of Thing Here

Daniel Fox

You get your cart.

You load it up with swabs, cloths, cleansing alcohol, ointments, salves, and bandages, just in case.

Off you go, toddling down the hushed carpeted hallways, giving a gentle knock on the doors. You help the residents get dressed. Or if they're bedridden, you wipe them down and help them fix their hair so they have some dignity, some pride, as they lie in place. A usual day in the faint peach hallways of the Rose Summit Hospice, out there in St. John's, Newfoundland.

What's *not* usual is entering Room 306 to find Archie Alby-Pinkerton doing deep knee bends, the few strands of his thin white hair flopping up and down with every drop and thrust, his bits and pieces also flopping around because he's naked, bellowing, "Do come in, Nurse Soriano! What's on the breakfast menu today, old girl? I'm absolutely hollow on the inside! Feed me, woman!"

This whole situation is not only unusual, it's downright surprising because at this time yesterday, Archie had been barely conscious and diagnosed as being about an hour away from death.

DID the in-house doctors line up to poke and prod at Archie? Did they ever! Tala and the other nurses did their best to keep the place from falling apart while the doctors were busy running every test they could think of on the old boy.

Round about 1 p.m., Tala took her lunch break, clustering with the other nurses in the little space out back, on the worn wooden park benches hidden away behind trellises. Tala spooned some of her chicken adobo onto Marge Cooper's plate, because Marge was a skinny thing and didn't eat near enough.

"Well?" said Marge.

"I get near the doctors," said Tala. "I hear them whispering that Archie's cancer is gone. *Gone* gone. Disappeared. Poof! All of it. Right now, they're arguing about whether or not they send him to the hospital for more tests or if they keep him for themselves, so they can figure out what's going on and get on the news."

Marge grinned. "They made me call all the night-shift nurses, ask them if they did anything special."

"Did they?"

"Nope. But Angela, she said she heard Archie muttering to himself all night long. When she went in to see him, he clammed up and told her to get lost."

"Maybe he was praying. Some people are private about that sort of thing."

"Archibald Alby-Pinkerton praying?" Marge snorted.

"If Archie ever talked to God, he'd treat him like an inferior."

"That's not nice."

"Maybe not, but true. He's a nasty old man. Look up the history of his business dealings sometime. It reads like Lucifer's résumé, all the people he hurt. Of all the people in this place, he's the very last one I'd waste a miracle on." Marge took a small bite of adobo. "Speaking of miracles, oh my God that's so good."

TALA GOT her back up whenever somebody called an elderly person mean. *You* sit around facing death all of your waking moments and then try being pleasant.

When she was growing up, back in the Philippines, Tala's grandmother had lived with them. Tala had watched as that fiery old lady's body had withered, even as her mind stayed sharp, a bright bird caught in a shrinking cage. She had cared for that beloved old woman as best she could, but there were some battles that were never going to hand you a win.

By the time her family had come over to Canada, Tala was destined to become a hospice nurse. And God help you if you denigrated the elderly within her earshot. Except... it turned out that maybe, just this once, Marge was right.

As there were no computers kicking around in 1973 for you to look up information, after her shift ended, Tala hustled her buns over to the library and did a bunch of digging into Archie's past. She knew Archie had to have money. You didn't land in a swank joint like the Rose Summit Hospice with its built-in bar, huge swimming pool and sweeping views of the coast if you only had two nickels to rub together.

But it was *how* Archie earned all of his money.

He was born pretty rich, son of a furniture-company tycoon. When he was twenty-eight, he formed his own company that helped struggling Canadian businesses. But instead of helping them, Archie's company would cut staff and sell off equipment. When the company inevitably went under, Archie's company would get first dibs on the sales of all remaining assets. Tala couldn't figure out how any of this was legal, or why anybody would hire Archie's company after the first time this happened, but that was it. That was how he had made his billions on top of his inheritance.

That did sound a little on the nasty side.

The real kicker was a quote she found from about twenty years earlier. A newspaper reporter had asked Archie about the government's efforts to battle poverty. There was a picture of Archie, twenty years younger, his head covered in thick white hair, smiling at the camera over his bow tie. The quote he gave was, word for word, "Poverty? Poverty is a social good. The more people with empty bellies, the more people we have working their tails off to get to the top."

Tala came from poverty. She knew the strain and the fear of it. You didn't work your tail off to "get to the top"— you worked it off just to survive. And if that quote didn't set steam boiling out of her ears, then you don't know Tala Soriano very well.

Still, at Tala's core, she knew that the old boy had to be afraid of death. And that was a terrible fear indeed. No matter how nasty and mean he was, she'd find the little speck of goodness in him and hold onto that as she helped ease him on the way to his next journey.

Or that was the plan, anyway.

Except, the next morning when Tala wheeled in the great big breakfast he had ordered, Archie eyed her and said, "How'd you like to make $10,000?"

She lifted his tray off the cart and put it on the stand across his bed. She caught him trying to look down her top. "Do I get to keep my dignity?"

"Dignity? Dignity is synonymous with being an absolute bore, doll. Tell me your definition of the word."

"It's self-respect. It's acting like a higher version of yourself."

Archie dipped a piece of toast in his egg yolk. "Now just between you and me and the bedspread here, does any of that really sound better than the life a billionaire can give you? You're a good-looking Mex girl…"

"Filipino. I'm from the Philippines."

He flapped a dismissive hand at her. "Potato po-tah-to. The point is…" he lifted his tray and pointed down at where his blanket had developed a tent shape, "…look who's back in town!"

Tala was finding it a bit of a chore to find that little diamond of goodness in this man. She was about to tell him so using words that would have made her mother wash her mouth out with soap, but there was a knock at the door and Doctor Lennox stuck his head in.

The doctor was a wee little fellow: bald, with round glasses and ears that stuck straight out from the sides of his head. He blinked like a mole exposed to daylight, and then said, "I'm terribly sorry to disturb you, Mr. Alby-Pinkerton, but I'm afraid I have some bad news."

Archie's grin slid from his face, and he said something very strange. "It can't be my health. It's impossible that it's my health."

The doctor said, "Oh no, oh my, certainly not. It's an acquaintance of yours. Christopher Hutton? I'm afraid there's been a terrible car accident. He's dead."

"Oh." Archie didn't bother hiding a rather big sigh of relief as he shoved bacon in his mouth. "I thought something had gone wrong."

———

IT'S *impossible that it's my health.*

That line by Archie rolled around in Tala's mind that whole evening as she sat in her apartment trying to watch her shows. It was the *confidence* the old boy had displayed while saying that line.

How could you be so sure about your health after you'd had cancer as an unwelcome tenant for the past ten years?

She wanted to relax, but her brain just kept gnawing at this weirdness like a hungry little beaver. Around 7 p.m., she called in to the hospice and got Angela on the phone.

"Hey hon" said Angela, raucous noises coming through the line along with her voice. "That's Archie in the rec room. He's got a party going on in there. We keep having to tell him to stop yelling at people for leaving when they want to go to bed."

"Marge said you heard him muttering something last night, right?"

"Uh-huh, that's right. Took me a bit by surprise, because you know what he was like the past few days. He was more drugs than man, hadn't heard him say boo in a month at least. But last night, he sounded like he was having a full-on conversation. Now me, I thought maybe he was having one of those life-flashes-before-your-eyes moments, like he was seeing his mom hovering in the air above him and he was talking to her, that sort of thing. So what did I do?"

"You popped in."

"Right as rain. Popped my head right in. There was Archie sitting up in bed, which was a wonder in itself, with this big grin on his face. Looked like the cat that swallowed the canary, you ask me. I asked him who he had been talking to, and he told me to take a hike. Called me a 'withered old bat.' Like he's one to talk."

"Did you hear anything he was saying before you entered his room?"

"Nope. It was muffled by the door. And what I did hear, it sounded all foreign-like, y'know?"

"Anything else?"

"He wouldn't let me put his book away."

"Oh yeah? What was he reading?"

"It was a big thing in cracked black leather. Like a ledger. You'd think I'd asked to throw his baby out the window, the way he acted when I tried to take…" Angela's voice exploded in Tala's ear. "Archie! Buford can go to bed when Buford darn well pleases!"

"Is Archie going to bed anytime soon?"

"I should be so lucky. *ARCHIE!*"

There was a click, and then the dial tone.

Tala was in her car less than five minutes later.

ARCHIE WAS STILL at it in the rec room. He was yelling loud enough to be heard all the way down the hall, telling people to, "Get on up off your baggy behinds and dance, dammit!"

Tala slipped into Archie's room. He was on the top floor, with a fantastic view of the coast. The suite was twice the size of her apartment and featured a small kitchen space that Archie had never used. Furniture that cost more than her car was lined up around the walls, and she suspected that the paintings on the wall were originals. No prints for Mr. Alby-Pinkerton, thank you very much.

She zipped around the room. His dresser drawers: no black leather mystery book. His closet: ditto.

She checked under the bed. Under the mattress. In the bathroom.

The music from the rec room cut off.

Tala checked her watch, saw that it was nearly 9 p.m. Bedtime for a lot of the residents. Archie might be making his way down the hall right that very moment.

Think think think!

The only place she hadn't checked was the small kitchen area. Archie didn't cook; he had everything sent up from the main kitchen. She checked the cupboards. No mystery book.

There was a plastic jug of fruit punch in the fridge. Nothing at all in the freezer except ice cubes.

She yanked open the oven door. There it was. A large book bound in black leather with brass-tipped corners. She pulled it out and opened it up and got herself a head full of confusion.

It was a sketchbook. But there were no sketches. At least, not of the usual stuff like human studies or birds or fruit bowls. About three quarters of the pages were full of charcoal etchings, but what the etchings were supposed to be... she couldn't make heads or tails of it.

They were all variations of the same images. Common to all the pages was a large circle. The circle was filled and surrounded with weird symbols or letters or what were those thingies on walls in ancient Egypt? Hieroglyphs! Kind of like cute little pictures in place of words, except these hieroglyphs were anything but cute. They looked like people screaming in pain with their backs broken in half and their hands thrown up in despair. It was page after page of the circle, with different symbols and hieroglyphs.

The last page of the sketches looked like most of the other pages except, when she leaned her head in close, in kind of smelled like sulphur. She didn't have time to puzzle that one out because at that moment, she heard Archie not too far down the hall, calling out a hearty hello to someone.

She slipped the sketchbook back into the oven and exited the room lickety-split. Lucky for her, Archie was distracted by Doctor Lennox, who was adjusting his glasses and looking like he was this close to crying.

Archie was cuffing the doctor on his upper arm and saying, "Come on, Doc! Out with it!"

Tala slipped through to the far stairwell, pushing on the door oh-so-gently as she heard Doctor Lennox say, "I'm sorry to have to be the one to tell you, but I'm afraid another of your acquaintances, Zachary Bolland. has been involved in a terrible accident."

Archie sounded bored as all get out when he replied, "You don't say?"

TALA SPENT the next morning at work slipping past Archie's groping hands. All of the female staff did. This being back in the 70s, there wasn't any sort of HR department to complain to.

Archie was looking better than he had the day before. Tala could have sworn that his white hair was coming back in. It was thick enough now to hint at waves. The wattles of his neck had tightened. He wasn't a spring chicken by any means, but he also no longer moved like he was made of glass.

And of course, there was the ongoing mystery of his vanished tumours.

Something real odd was going on, no ifs, ands, or buts about it.

Tala nearly threw herself at the exit doors when her shift was over. She headed right back to the library and spent a fruitless hour trying to find something that would explain those weird symbols in Archie's sketchbook. She recreated them from memory as best she could on the back of one of the hospice's dining room menus, and used her drawing as a reference as she flipped through all sorts of books about the history of magic and ancient symbols and whatever else she could think of, all to no avail.

Tala gave up and was heading for the exit when she saw the newspaper racks. She gathered up a couple of the papers, wondering about the two men who had died over the past couple of days: Christopher Hutton and Zachary something-or-other. Whoever they were, Archie hadn't seemed particularly impressed by their untimely demises.

She found news about both of them quick enough. They were big business tycoons, just like Archie. They had both been around Archie's age. Christopher Hutton had inherited a transportation business. He owned fleets of those big containers that trains and transport ships lugged around the world. Zachary Bolland had something to do with importing industrial chemicals.

Zachary Bolland's write-up showed a picture from way back, somewhere in the early 1900s, of a trio of young men and one woman at some kind of black-tail party, arms around each other, free hands raising glasses of champagne in a toast. The caption said they were Christopher Hutton, Archie Alby-Pinkerton, Zachary Bolland, and Phillipa Rexley.

They had looked close as peas in a pod. Now two of them were dead in the span of two days, with a third seemingly getting younger and ditching his deadly medical condition. As for Phillipa Rexley, a quick look in the phone book showed she still lived right there in good old St. John's, not very far at all from the hospice.

PHILLIPA REXLEY'S house was nice, but not *holy-crap-wow* nice. Tala had been expecting a mansion. Instead she parked in front of a pretty two-storey red-brick house with bright white trim and black iron railings around the long front yard.

Miss Rexley answered the door herself. Her shining white hair was twisted into a braid that ran down her back. She stood in the doorway with the aid of a wooden cane and didn't seem inclined to let Tala in until Tala showed her the drawing she had made of Archie's weird sketchbook symbols.

"Oh Lord," she said, "is he still at that?" And then she

stood to the side and waved Tala in. "They were my boys," said Miss Rexley, once they had settled themselves on opposite ends of the softest couch Tala had ever encountered in her life. "We were the four musketeers, kicking up a fuss wherever we went. Archie though, nothing was ever fuss enough for him. He was the one who always wanted to race cars faster, drink more expensive champagne, dance until the sun came up. Eventually, even the high life wasn't high enough for him, and off he toddled, looking for something more." She pointed the end of her cane at the drawing Tala was holding in her hand. "That's when he got into all that stuff."

"It's black magic, isn't it?"

"Demonology, to be specific. I never believed it was real. But it was fun. We ran around in black robes holding daggers, chanting stuff in Latin. For a bunch of bored rich kids, it was an absolute riot."

"Archie believes in it. What's more, I think he finally got it to work. Two days ago, he was inches from death. He had multiple forms of cancer making a banquet out of his insides. He was heard chanting, and the next day the cancer was gone. *Gone* gone. The day after that, he was up on his feet running around trying to pinch all us nurses on our backsides. And something else happened in those two days."

"Chris and Zach died." Miss Rexley got up and began to pace. Tala could see it was hurting her, probably arthritis in the hips from the way she moved. "So we're believing in demons now?"

"And the bargains men make with them for some extra time here on Earth."

"But the cost... sacrificing his only friends in the world?"

"I guess I came here hoping you'd tell me that he would never do such a thing."

Miss Rexley sat again, closer to Tala. "At our age, we're looking Death in the face every day. We can smell her perfume, we can feel her breath on our faces, always. If I was able to make a bargain with a demon for more time, for youth again..."

"Even if it meant sacrificing people who cared for you?"

Miss Rexley shook her head. "No, I don't suppose I would."

"But Archie?"

"Archie was always a very driven man. Don't go looking for goodness in him, Miss..."

"'Tala' does me just fine."

"That is a lovely name. Don't hope for goodness in Archie. The greatest joys he ever experienced in life came from when he was being the most cruel. When I decided to give away most of my family's fortune to various charities, he damn near throttled me to try to get me to stop."

"I hope you're wrong."

"Me too. It would be nice to think we all contain at least a speck of goodness in us, eh? Speaking of goodness, I have a charity function tonight. Books for children. So, I must dash."

Tala said her goodbyes but then turned back at the front door and held up the drawing. "One last question, real quick. Is this thing for one demon in particular, or is it more of a one-size-fits-all kind of thing?"

"Oh, he's an ancient Middle Eastern fellow. Mean bugger by the name of Chayateen. He feeds on cruelty."

TALA DROVE BACK to the hospice because she didn't think there was much chance of her sleeping, knowing a crank like Archie Alby-Pinkerton was having chats with a demon that loved a good bit of cruelty. That was just the kind of thing that really messed up the old circadian rhythm.

She knocked on Archie's door around 7 p.m. and heard his cheerful voice yell, "What?!" She entered to find him packing up his belongings into cardboard boxes. He looked better than ever. He appeared to be fifty at most, probably even younger, and the grey polo shirt showed tight muscles moving as he hefted a box.

"Hey cutie-pie," he said. "Did you drop that inconvenient desire for dignity yet?"

Tala opened her mouth to reply that the gig was up, she knew all about the demon Chayateen and how Archie was feeding his friends to the thing in exchange for renewed youth, but before she could get any of that out, Doctor Lennox shuffled in and said, "I'm afraid I have bad news yet again, Mr. Alby-Pinkerton. Your friend, Miss Phillipa Rexley, she was at a charity event, and a bookcase fell over and crushed her."

Archie said, "Hey chief, I'm going to need more packing tape."

TALA WALKED along the pebble shoreline down from the hospice. There were lights from cargo ships out there, and she got to wondering if she could swim even half the distance from here to their rusty hulls. She took a couple of steps towards the water when she heard pebbles crunch behind her. Doctor Lennox was making his way in her direction, struggling to light a pipe in the wind.

He stopped when he saw her. "Well! Haven't seen you down here before."

"You come here often?"

"When I need to clear my head. And these past couple of days... whew!"

"So Archie is leaving?"

"Yes. Most of the doctors would prefer that he'd stay so we can study him right down to his atoms. I suppose he is a miracle, after all."

Tala wasn't so sure she'd call it that. "What about you?"

"Between you and me..." the doctor looked around to spot out any eavesdroppers, "he gives me the creeps. There's something about that fellow that just isn't right. In the space of three days, I've had to tell him that three of his friends have died. Did he even blink an eye? No, he certainly did not." The doctor gave up on his pipe and shoved it into his pocket. "It's like he didn't feel a thing."

If metaphors manifested as reality, the doctor would have seen a great big light bulb go *bing!* above Tala's head.

"Doc!" she shouted, "you're beautiful!"

Before the doctor could ask why she would think such a thing, she had sprinted halfway back up to the hospice.

―――――

SHE DIDN'T BOTHER KNOCKING at Archie's door this time; she just went straight on in.

"I want to see him."

Archie, who was busy combing his thick greying locks in

the mirror, spun around like a hornet had just stung his backside. "Who?"

"Your demon pal Chayateen, that's who. I know all about how you and your bored rich-kid buddies played around with demonology and you finally got it to work and you made a bargain with him to feed him deaths in exchange for youth. So chop-chop, whip him on up."

"You're so interested in deals with devils, you can make one with me. I'll call him, but you have to go on a date with me."

"Oh geez, fine. Whatever. Just get 'er done, huh?"

Archie ran over to close the door behind her. He then ran back and hunted through one of the cardboard boxes and pulled out the old black leather sketchbook. He flipped to the final sketch and laid it on the small round table near the kitchen.

He started chanting. The words weren't Latin, Tala was pretty sure of that, but they sure sounded old. No, not *sounded...* they *felt* old. And sour. And pretty slobbery. Archie spit a whole bunch pronouncing them, and that was pretty gross.

The shaded area inside of the big circle on the page seemed to fall away into a greenish-black space that smelled of rotten eggs. Archie leaned down and called out, "Hey Chayateen, shake a leg, huh?"

The empty whirling green nothingness suddenly had a shadow in it, and the shadow came racing closer and closer until it filled the circle. A great big muscular arm thrust out of the circle into the room, scaly and ending in talons, and the hand slammed down on the table.

"You've summoned me *again?*" said a deep voice that kind of sounded like its owner was underwater.

"Yeah pal, won't take long." Archie gestured at the arm with a *ta-da!* motion and looked at Tala. "There ya go. Do you like Italian food or…"

"What's that?" said Tala.

"What do you mean 'What's that'? It's an ancient demon."

The arm raised and waved. "Hey," said the voice.

"That's an arm, not a demon," said Tala.

"Thank you!" said Chayateen. "Leave it to big brains over here," the long green index finger pointed around, trying to find Archie, "to draw a summoning circle only big enough to fit my arm."

"Ex-cuse *me*," said Archie. "I had to fit the summoning circle in a sketchbook. Sorry I wasn't able to draw chalk marks all over the floor while I was busy, you know, *dying*."

The deep voice sighed. "Why am I here this time? You want me to rewind you right back to the embryonic stage?"

"Actually, that's what I wanted to see you about," said Tala, daring to take a step closer. "The deals you made with Archie to get his youth back."

"What about them?" said the demon.

"You feed off cruelty, don't you? You needed Archie to pick the people closest to him as the price for his youth. Because it would hurt him the most to give up people he cared about."

"Yes," said the demon. "That is so."

"Well…" said Tara, stepping closer still, "aren't you still feeling a little bit peckish?"

"Peckish?" said the demon, its arm raised in a possible shrugging gesture. "I'm famished! I *starve*, human!"

"Well I gotta tell ya, Mr. Chayateen sir, I think that's

maybe because you made a deal with just the worst possible fella."

"How do you mean?"

"Archie here got informed three times that his child-hood friends died, bing-bang-boom, one after another, and he hasn't shed a single tear. He didn't sigh, he didn't groan, he didn't so much as blink. He didn't care. He didn't feel a thing. You can't force cruel decisions on a man who is himself full of cruelty. I hate to tell you, big guy, but I think you kind of got ripped off."

There was an awkward, sulphur-scented silence.

Then the hand reared up, made a fist, and slammed back down on the table hard enough to make the whole thing jump. "Archibald Alby-Pinkerton! You have wronged me!"

"Whoa whoa whoa," said Archibald, holding up his own hands in a placating gesture. "Who are you going to believe? Me or some wage-slave broad who…"

"I HUNGER!"

"I think I can fix that for you, boss," said Tala. "Because I tell ya, I've spent my whole life trying to find the best in everybody. The last three days, dealing with this whole thing with Archie, I've just searched and searched and searched, and I haven't found a single ounce of decency in this man. Lord knows I've tried. And the Lord also knows I've never wanted to have dealings with a demon. But I'm willing to make you a deal now. I'll choose to give you Archibald in exchange for you giving that nice Miss Phillipa Rexley back the rest of her natural lifespan, even if it's just a day."

"What is this?" said Archie. "What are we even talking about here? You can't choose a nurse over me!"

"Why not?" said the demon.

"Because I'm rich!"

"I'm going to feel awful about making this deal for the rest of my life," said Tala, turning to Archie, "because I failed to find any good in you. I'm so sorry." Tala turned to the demon's arm. "How does my sadness taste?"

"Delicious!" roared the demon.

There was a pop, the sound of air rushing to fill a vacuum, and Archie wasn't there anymore.

ON THE OTHER side of town, Phillipa Rexley, who had suffered a serious case of broken neck-itis, suddenly sat up in the back of an ambulance.

"It's a miracle!" said the paramedic.

Interlopers in the Temple

Elizabeth Hosang

A rustle in the trees behind him made Josiah turn his head, one hand gripping the hilt of his sword.

Following him, Eril jumped, pulling his dagger out of its sheath. "What is it?" the boy asked.

Josiah scanned the path behind them. This far from the village the predators ruled the forest unchecked, and burdened as he was with the annual offering to the Oracle of the Temple, he could not afford to be attacked.

After a moment's hesitation, he realized that the wind was blowing towards him from the direction of the sound. "It's nothing. No predator would attack from upwind."

"Are you sure?" Eril asked, jerking his dagger nervously as he looked around.

Josiah released his grip on his sword. "I am a hunter. I would know if we were being stalked." He looked up, marking the location of the sun in the sky. "We need to hurry if we are to be back before sundown."

The pilgrims resumed their journey. They had set out before sunrise, travelling the familiar roads through the cultivated orchards and farmlands that their people had carved out of the forest years ago. By the time the sun rose they had reached the borders of the village's territory, pausing only long enough to exchange greetings with the guardians at the gate. The village had existed for many generations before building the wall that separated it from the monsters in the forest. Since then, the village had prospered, spared from attacks by the things with glowing eyes and death-dealing claws that roamed the forest.

By mid-morning, they had traversed the densest part of the forest. The trees were sparser here as the trail began to rise. Josiah paused to shift the heavy pack on his back to balance it better as he began the climb. Behind him, Eril panted and pulled out a water skin.

"Save your water," Josiah told him. "You will need it after our ascent. This part of the trail is steep, but Master Kinu showed me how to climb it during my first days of training as Guardian." Master Kinu had said that when the day came that he could no longer climb the trail, it would be time to hand over guardianship to Josiah.

"Watch me carefully. The key to this climb is to know which rocks in the dirt are solid footholds, and which are loose in the red soil and will give way underfoot."

Eril's expression was sullen, but he put the water skin away and bowed his head, as befit an apprentice.

The sun was near its zenith when Josiah crested the slope and paused to catch his breath. Turning, he extended his hand to assist Eril up the last few feet. As soon as he reached the level ground, Eril pulled his hand free and collapsed to his knees, taking out his water skin and gulping from it.

"Save some for the return journey," Josiah cautioned,

taking out his own skin and sipping from it. "Do you remember the first verse of the incantation that grants access to the Temple portal?"

"Yes, Master," Eril grumbled in reply. "I don't know why I had to come with you. The offering is small enough that you don't need my assistance to carry it."

"You are here to learn the ways of the Guardian, just as I learned from Master Kinu."

The younger man rolled his eyes, and Josiah turned away so the boy would not see him clench his fists in frustration. Eril was the youngest son of a village elder with whom Josiah had frequently clashed. The boy was willful and accustomed to others deferring to him. Josiah could not afford to show weakness in front of him.

Alas, the boy was not wrong. This season the crops had been meagre, and the villagers had been loath to part with the food required for the offering. Even the cattle were thin, and the elders had refused to part with the portion of meat specified in the Scrolls of the Guardian.

If Master Kinu had been here, Josiah's pack would not be so light. Master Kinu had commanded the respect of the village. He had been a powerful speaker, a mover of men. Unfortunately, a sudden summer storm had weakened the riverbanks, destroying the pier. Master Kinu had been swept away while trying to save fishermen caught out in the open when the storm broke. While Josiah was an experienced hunter and had been trained in the rituals of the Temple, he had not yet been taught the art of persuasion. Master Kinu had explained that persuasion was something that could not be taught in a classroom. It could only be taught by watching and listening, much to Josiah's frustration. He had experienced only two seasons training with

Master Kinu instead of the ten seasons normally spent as an apprentice. Josiah was certain that this was yet another reason the village elders had refused to give him all that was expected for the seasonal offering. In his memory he could hear again the voice of Eril's father, Orial, the town master, telling him that if the Oracle of the Temple were really watching over the village, then He would know that the crops had been poor this year, and would understand why the offering was meagre.

When Josiah became Guardian, Orial had insisted that Josiah take Eril as his apprentice. Instead of a helper, Josiah found himself burdened with a spy who watched him intently, reporting back any misstep.

"It is time to continue our journey," Josiah said. Eril looked into Josiah's eyes and took another long drink from his water skin before sealing it and stowing it back in his own light pack. Slowly he rose to his feet, then nodded his head slightly instead of executing a full bow, still staring defiantly at Josiah.

Josiah turned around and pushed a tall plant aside from his path, gripping it hard in his anger. The sensation of the leafy stalk ripping in his hand caused him to stop and take a few deep breaths, as he had been taught, to let go of his fury. It was not his fault that he was so young and inexperienced. It was not his fault that Master Kinu had selected a lowly hunter as an apprentice instead of one of the more educated sons of the village elders. It was not his fault that Master Kinu had died unexpectedly, leaving his education unfinished. He had been trained in the rituals to ensure that the river water ran clean where it entered their reservoir, and he had ensured good health for all who drank from it. Surely that marked him as a worthy successor to Kinu, even if his beard was not silvered and his words were not wise? He was good with his hands; that had always been enough until he had been named apprentice.

Josiah's hand moved to his chest, patting the pouch that hung beneath his jerkin. It contained the scroll with the prayers and supplications he would make on behalf of the village, asking for the blessing of the Oracle. Josiah had laboured for two days preparing the scrolls, working frantically to determine the correct invocation to avoid the Oracle's wrath, explaining the wording to Eril as he worked. The boy had corrected Josiah from time to time, even offering to write out the invocation in his more elegant script, taking every opportunity to remind Josiah of his superior education.

Josiah had ground his teeth, mindful of Master Kinu's lessons on humility, and accepted the help. There had been illness in the village this year that carried off two hunters in the prime of their lives, and three women were heavy with child. Without the blessing of the Oracle, the village would know much loss. For its sake he had sacrificed his pride and endured the younger man's scornful looks.

At last, Master and Apprentice broke through the trees and stood at the edge of the clearing at the base of another cliff. "We're here," Josiah whispered reverently.

Beside him, Eril looked around but seemed unimpressed. "Where's the Temple?"

Josiah pointed up to the top of the cliff.

"Why don't we just go up there directly?" Eril said, pointing to a narrow path to the side of the stone wall that led up a steep incline.

The former huntsman spun angrily, grabbing the younger man by the arm and jerking him around so they were face-to-face. "Do not speak blasphemy in this sacred place! The Temple is His sacred abode, and this glade is the place where He deigns to speak to us. We are here to beg favour for our village. You will show respect for me, and for our mission, and if you cannot do that, then you will at least stand here and remain silent." Eril's eyes were wide with shock, but for once his mouth stayed closed.

Josiah crossed the clearing to a solid rock face, apparently unbroken. He set his pack on the ground and untied it. Reverently, he laid out the vessels he carried. Bowing before them, he reached into his jerkin and pulled out the incantation, unrolling it with trembling hands. Rising to his feet, he stood before the sheer grey stone and began to read.

"Oh Great Oracle of the Temple, I come before you as Guardian of the Village of the Riverside. Begin provisioning upload."

An opening appeared in the cliff face and the voice of the Oracle replied to him. "Present provisions to be uploaded." Out of the corner of his eye, Josiah noted with satisfaction that Eril's mouth had dropped open at the disembodied voice.

Josiah lifted the three earthenware jars filled with beer. He placed them reverently into the alcove and stood back. "Liquid provisions: alcohol, three gallons." He held his breath as the door to the alcove slid down. The containers were sized as specified by the sacred scrolls, but there were two fewer than the scrolls required.

After what felt like the length of many seasons, the alcove opened again. Anxiously, Josiah placed a parcel of fresh meat wrapped in vine leaves into the recess. Along with the sacred scrolls, Master Kinu had left him two stones and a balance. The measure of meat was supposed to match the weight of the two stones, but once again, Josiah carried less than was called for. "Beef, weight unknown." The alcove door closed, and again Josiah waited for the wrath of the Oracle to be visited upon him. Once more, the door opened without comment.

Josiah removed the final parcel from his pack: a woven basket containing fruits and vegetables. There should have been two of them, filled to the brim with the finest crops the village had to offer. Instead, there were a few meagre root vegetables and small fruits, some showing signs of worms. With trembling hands, he placed this paltry offering into the alcove. "Produce, weight unknown." The door slid down.

As he waited for the Oracle's judgement, Josiah swallowed the supplications that came to his lips. He longed to fall on his knees, to explain about the poor harvest, to beg understanding for his youth and lack of training, to make excuses about failed crops and arrogant elders so accustomed to the gifts of the Oracle that they would deny Him proper sacrifice. All these things he would have said and more, but Master Kinu had explained to him that contact with the Oracle must follow a set script—to deviate from it was to risk the Oracle's anger. And he would not debase himself while Eril watched.

At last the alcove opened, the Oracle awaiting the final words of the first part of the spell. Clenching his fists to stop them shaking, Josiah forced the sacred words from his lips. "Upload complete."

Another long moment, and then the Oracle spoke again. "Upload verified. Specify required supplies."

The Oracle had forgiven him! Josiah nearly wept with

relief. With trembling hands he held up the scroll and unrolled it to the next part of the incantation. He took a deep breath and began.

"Water filter replacements: size sixty millimetres, quantity four." He paused for a moment, waiting for the words which would signify that the Oracle had accepted his entreaty.

"Acknowledged. Specify additional supplies."

"Vaccines: infant inoculations, six." Along with the three expected infants, there were two young children born recently in the village, whose arrival had not been foreseen at the Time of Offering last year. For this reason, Josiah had decided to ask for an additional blessing in case the same thing happened again.

"Acknowledged. Specify additional supplies."

"Vaccines: adult inoculations; tetanus boosters, twenty." The two hunters who had died in their prime had been overdue for their blessing. Josiah was determined that this would not happen again.

"Acknowledged. Specify additional supplies."

Josiah hesitated. Surely the Oracle would not grant all that he requested after such a meagre offering? Still, Master Kinu had told him that hesitation when facing the Oracle would only fail those who relied on Josiah as Guardian. "Batteries: lithium, twelve." These last items were the least important. They were the fuel that fed the strange device that kept the predators away from the wall. Josiah had never understood why the villagers had used the device. Surely their wall was sufficient in the night? Nonetheless, feeding the device was part of his duties as Guardian. If he was supposed to keep the device happy, he would. But he had left this request until last. If the Oracle was angry at the meagreness of their offerings, perhaps He would at least grant the other items.

"Acknowledged. Specify additional supplies."

Saying a silent prayer of thanks, Josiah rolled up his Spell of Supplication and bowed to the alcove. "Request complete." With trembling hands, he tucked the scroll inside his jerkin and waited.

"Download commencing: water filter replacements." Josiah nearly leapt with joy as the voice of the Oracle announced the arrival of the requested gifts. With a woosh the door to the alcove rose, revealing a small box. Josiah grabbed it with trembling hands and opened the flaps. Inside, sat four shiny tubes of a material called mesh, enough to ensure that the village had safe drinking water for another year. Josiah placed the box in his pack and continued the spell.

"Supplies received."

The door closed and Josiah waited.

"Vaccines: infant inoculations, adult inoculations, tetanus boosters." The door opened again, displaying a green chest with rounded edges and a handle. Josiah took the box gently from the opening and knelt, placing the chest on his pack. With trembling hands, he undid the latches and opened it. Inside, on a strange black cushion, rested twenty-six gleaming tubes, with coloured stripes on their ends denoting their contents. Each of these blessings had the power to prevent disease, when pressed against the arm of a person. Once used, the tubes were worn as jewelry by the recipient, marking them as protected against the evil spirits who came in the night and stole a baby's breath or froze a person's limbs until even breathing ceased. Josiah closed the chest and reverently secured the latches. Only after stowing the precious cargo in his pack did he realize that the alcove door was still open.

"Supplies received." The door closed and Josiah remained on his knees, uncertain of whether the final boon would be granted.

"Batteries: lithium." The door opened again and Josiah grabbed the case lest the Oracle change His mind. He stowed the case and bowed low to the ground.

"Supplies received."

"Acknowledged. Resupply mission completed." The door closed, sealing the opening.

The ritual was complete. The offerings had been accepted and the boons granted. He knew he was not supposed to linger in the clearing, but in gratitude Josiah murmured a small prayer of thanksgiving.

A strange noise intruded on his meditation. It took Josiah a minute to place the sound: men cheering. Josiah sat up abruptly and looked at Eril. The younger man was also looking around in confusion. The village was far from this place, and climbing the sacred mountain was forbidden to anyone other than the Guardian or his apprentice. Another cheer sounded. Josiah leapt to his feet, one hand on his walking stick, the other on the hilt of his sword. It was bad enough that the elders denied him what was needed for the sacrifice. Surely none of them had the audacity to follow him?

The wind shifted, and the birds in the trees grew silent. Josiah waited, years of training as a hunter enabling him to still his laboured breath and racing heartbeat. He waited, all senses open, like a predator scenting the wind.

It couldn't be. The voices were not coming from behind him. They were coming from further up the mountain.

They were coming from the Temple! Josiah trembled with rage. Who dared enter the Temple, where even the guardians were forbidden to tread? Josiah crossed the clearing to the start of the forbidden path and began to climb. Behind him, Eril struggled to follow. The path was steep, but short. It curved around to stop at what appeared to be another wall resembling the cliff face with the offering alcove. Unsure what to do next, Josiah searched his memories of lessons with Master Kinu. "O Great Oracle, I, a lowly Guardian, request access to the Temple."

After a moment he heard footsteps approaching from the other side of the stone wall. When it opened, Josiah recoiled in surprise. Instead of a leather-clad member of the village, here stood a man in baggy green clothes, with oddly coloured patches on the chest and shoulders. His boots were heavy and black, with a string that zigzagged across the top and thick soles of a material Josiah had never seen before. Around his waist was a black belt that held a strange black pouch at his hip. From the pouch emerged an oddly shaped black chunk that gleamed in a way similar to the water filters. Josiah did not know what the black thing did, but from its position, so like the placement of his own sword, Josiah guessed that it was the handle to a blade or some other weapon. The man did not have the bearing of a hunter, however. Instead, he had the rough stubble and the bleary eyes that came with too much beer consumed too quickly.

"Hey, lookit this. It's a native." The man belched, his foul breath washing over Josiah. "No, wait, it's two! Now it's a party!"

"Really?" Another man staggered into view. He wore the same strange clothing, with the same heavy footwear that clomped as he walked. "Whaddya know, it's the wait-ers! I told you that stuff was fresh. Got any more?"

Josiah stood immobile, his mind reeling as he took in these strange men. There was nothing in the sacred scrolls that suggested there was more than one Oracle in the Temple. Everything he had ever read or been taught said that the Oracle was not a being like him. The Oracle was a creature beyond the understanding of the humble villagers, not to be approached or invoked except through the sacred alcove. These creatures, despite their strange dress and ill manners, were clearly men like himself. What were they doing here?

"Buddy! You okay there?" The man who had appeared first was peering at him strangely, while the other had gone back into the Temple.

"C'mon in, take a load off." The man who had opened the door stepped outside, put one arm around Josiah's shoulders and another around Eril's, and pulled them into a large room. Terror gripped Josiah and he fell to the ground, his face pressed to the floor in horror. Entering the Temple was punishable by death.

"Anders! You know the rules! We're not supposed to interact with the locals. Get them out of here and shut the door."

"Ah, come on, Sarge. It's just a couple of primitives. What's the harm?"

"The harm is, we follow protocol. Refueling stations are maintained by the locals on the condition that we don't interact with them."

"Geeze. If I'd wanted to follow rules I'd have stayed in the marines. I thought joining a private military organiza-tion would be more relaxed."

The strange words flowing over his head were like a storm wind buffeting Josiah; he was aware of them but their meaning eluded him. Finally, one word resonated with him: locals. They were discussing him. He raised his head cautiously, avoiding the eyes of the men around him. Next to him Eril was still on his feet, looking around in wonder. A table filled one corner of the room, and another two men sat at it. Most of them wore rough beards or stubble. Only the hunters in his village wore beards, and none would leave them as ragged as these. Nor would even the most lowly in his village allow themselves to be as poorly groomed or as smelly as these men.

He looked around. There were no windows, yet light filled the room. It came from torches that did not flicker but shone steadily. Several shelves held strange devices.

"Stand up, son. I'm sorry, but you have to leave now." The man who had spoken with authority reached down and gripped Josiah under the arm, lifting him to his feet. This man was dressed like the others, but his eyes were clear and his face shaven. This man had the bearing of a leader.

"Well, thanks anyway." The second man to come to the door walked over to the table. He lifted a cup to his mouth and took a long drink before slamming it on the table. He reached forward and grabbed an earthen vessel, using it to refill his cup. Josiah stared at the vessel. It was identical to those he had loaded into the offertory alcove.

"What are you doing?" He lunged forward and grabbed the vessel from the table. "This is for the Oracle of the Temple. It is not for mere men. How dare you!"

"Hey!" The men sitting at the table jumped up and began shouting, anger focussing their bleary eyes. The neatly groomed one, Sarge, held up a hand, and the others went silent. All of them rested their hands on the strange weapons at their hips.

The one with authority spoke again. "At ease. Everyone just relax. Look, I'm sorry. We meant no disrespect. Just go on back to your village. We'll clean this up before the Oracle gets back."

"What's an Oracle?" one of the men asked.

"Oh, right. I know this." The one called Anders spoke. "That's the line the Company uses when it sets up these stations. They tell the locals there's some magic wizard living here. The locals provide food and drink, and the stations give them a few trinkets in return."

One of the others at the table snorted. "What, like glass beads?"

"Shut up, both of you," the leader hissed.

"Whatever," another man said. "I'm just glad we got a chance to eat everything fresh before the automated supply system turned it into that freeze-dried crap we normally get."

"Yeah, thanks, buddy," said the one called Anders. He clapped Josiah on the shoulder.

The impact of the man's hand finally broke through Josiah's horrified paralysis, releasing his rage. In one swift move he drew his sword and swung it upwards, slicing through Anders' throat. Another swing, and he thrust into the gut of the other man who had come to the door.

The man with authority had drawn his weapon and was raising it. Josiah leapt to him, smashed the hand holding the weapon to one side and drove his sword into the man's abdomen.

A sound like thunder rang through the Temple. The

two men behind the table were pointing their weapons at Josiah. He saw no blade, but ducked nonetheless. He shoved the table towards them, striking them in the waist and knocking them backwards. Another thunderclap rang through the Temple and one of the lights shattered, throwing off sparks. Josiah leapt onto the table and over it before the men could recover their balance. He struck one of them with his fist, knocking him backwards, while simultaneously stabbing the other. The man he had punched staggered back and fell on the ground, dropping his weapon. Josiah stood over him for a moment, the point of his blade at the man's throat. "Let no man defile the sacred Temple of the Oracle," he said, before cleaving the man's head from his shoulders.

He looked around at the bodies, to be certain that none moved. The only figure still on his feet was Eril. Eyes wide, face ashen, he stood immobile. Josiah stalked around the table towards his apprentice, blood dripping from his sword.

"You have something to say, Apprentice?"

Eril dropped to his knees. "No, Master."

THE NEXT MORNING, the two men set forth on the return journey. They had spent the rest of the previous day purifying the Temple. Eril had dragged the bodies outside and prepared them for burial as Josiah dug the graves in the woods that surrounded the Oracle's alcove. They had defiled the Temple, but they were men, after a sort, and Josiah felt that the Oracle would be happier if they were treated as such.

While it pained him to violate the Temple further, Josiah had searched until he found several jugs of the unpleasantly scented liquid that the villagers used to clean their blades after preparing meat. He stood watch as Eril scrubbed on his hands and knees. When the work was finished, the only trace of the violators of the Temple was the strong smell of the cleaner.

By the time they had buried the bodies and purified the Temple, it was close to dark. They dared not risk returning through the predators' forest until the next day. Instead, they slept outside the Temple at the threshold, Eril shivering in the dirt.

Now they were on their way back to the village; late, but with Eril bearing the requested blessings on his back. The younger man had lifted the pack without prompting, bowed his head when addressed, and replied "Yes, Master," when Josiah gave him orders.

Josiah led their trek with his head held high. The fight had reminded him that while he had not Master Kinu's gift for persuasion, he had his own gifts and his own way of serving the Oracle. Like Eril, the elders of the village would not defy him again.

Ladies Who Lunch

Abby Andresen

That's what you'd call tucking into your lunch, thought Liz, watching Carla methodically devour her James Dean, what this 1950s-style diner called their concoction of pulled pork, sunny-side up egg, black beans and sour cream, all piled into a burger bun.

After briefly getting caught up with each other and discussing the menu with its Velvet Elvis, Little Richard and Norma Jean sandwiches, they were out of conversation. After about ten years, nothing had changed except Carla's aging face. Liz sighed and cut into her huevos rancheros. She should have known she'd run into Carla at the Galleria, the upscale mall where Carla had a second home at Louis Vuitton. "Let's have lunch next week," Carla had decreed, and Liz, without good excuses because she only worked part time now, couldn't manage to say no.

"How's your James Dean?" offered Liz, watching Carla gobble a mouthful.

Carla chewed for a while as if considering it, then took

a long swig from her Chardonnay and swished it around in her mouth. "Good," she said and refocused on her plate.

"My eggs are good, too," said Liz to Carla's forehead.

At least the food was good. The eggs were fresh tasting, and the tortilla was warm and crispy. Liz was wearing a dress today to brighten the occasion, one on which she'd received several compliments. It was forest green crepe fabric and flared just below her knees, a nice look with her rust leather boots and silk scarf in muted oranges and greens. But Carla didn't seem to notice, and if she did notice she either didn't care or was withholding comment. Typical Carla. Miffed, Liz decided not to compliment Carla on her fluffy white sweater or on her silver necklace with the big turquoise stone. New from one of her cruises, probably.

Liz took a deep drink of Merlot, one of the few activities she had in common with Carla. But drinking buddies did not good lunching ladies make. As she always had with Carla, Liz scanned her mind for suitable shallow topics to talk about. Apparently, it was still her job to keep their dreary conversation going. Not politics. Carla wasn't even registered to vote, and from what Liz knew of her political views, that was a good thing. She didn't read either, and she had no interest in anything vintage, least of all the mid-century décor blog Liz co-edited. Liz had two reference book reviews overdue: one on art deco lamps, the other on Eames chairs, and she hadn't started either one of them.

"I have a lot of work to do this afternoon," Liz said, implying she couldn't dawdle. "A couple of books to review." Carla looked up, distracted by something behind Liz's back, then took a big bite of her James Dean. "Books" didn't register in Carla's brain. She might as well have said she was writing fairy tales, or a treatise on *Origin of the Species*, or a historical review of the *Ziegfeld Follies* from a feminist perspective.

Liz felt a creeping sense of entrapment. They were really packed together in this diner, a refurbished old railroad car with small, uncomfortable booths. The place was one of their old haunts. Carla, fond of the big sandwiches, still didn't want to lunch anywhere else.

"So is your shoulder still acting up?" Liz flung into the abyss. They'd both had a history of shoulder problems. It was the other thing they had in common.

Carla stopped chewing and looked up at her, blinking slowly, as if trying to recall her presence. She swallowed a mouthful that made the fleshy pouch under her chin bob, then cleared her throat with a moist rattle. "Oh, it still hurts sometimes," she sighed. "It's what they call frozen now. A frozen shoulder. Can you believe it? My doctor says to me, he says, 'You have a frozen shoulder.' And I'm thinking, I never heard of such a thing. It isn't cold at all. Anyways, they gave me some physical therapy and I have to do these exercises every day now. It's loosening up a little, but he says to me that the range of motion is still down 30 percent from normal."

"Oh, wow," said Liz. She sipped her Merlot and marvelled at what a piece of work Carla was. They never should have met. They never would have, if Liz's streak of ill-advised choices and bad luck hadn't washed her up at the bank ten years ago as an office temp. "You're mine," Carla had declared when she came to collect Liz from the lobby, her stout body clothed in a fabulous Chanel suit, so at odds with the bumpkin talk that came out of her mouth.

"I can't even reach behind me to scratch my own back,"

Carla mourned. "And I can't scrub my back in the shower even. So then, my doctor says to me I wasn't using my shoulder enough, that's why it got frozen. Well, I says to him right back, I says I wasn't using my shoulder enough because it hurt."

"Oh, ouch," said Liz, grateful to feel the first warm stirrings of her Merlot. Of course Carla had forgotten that she had shoulder problems, too. "My shoulder's a little better now that I'm not sleeping on it," Liz reminded her. She shrugged to show that she had one.

"Uh," said Carla around an open mouthful of very yellow egg, followed by more Chardonnay. A fragment of green garnish was sticking out of the side of Carla's wide mouth, as if she'd caught something in swampy terrain. Liz averted her eyes.

"How are you ladies doing?" asked the perky not-so-young server, dressed 1950s style in saddle shoes and ankle socks accented by incongruous piercings and tattoos. "Can I get you ladies anything? Another glass of wine?" Liz smiled at her, happy for the interruption.

They readily agreed to another round.

"Anyways," Carla continued after dismissing the server with a wave of her hand. "At least they probably won't have to operate on it, he says."

"That's good," Liz said. She stabbed at her huevos rancheros, wishing she was home working on her reviews. Hopefully the Merlot wouldn't make her too drowsy to write. Carla returned hungrily to her James Dean, shoving it in as if she hadn't eaten in days, even splattering some black beans on her white sweater.

"Oh no," said Liz, motioning with her napkin because

Carla appeared oblivious. "Looks like you spilled on your sweater there."

Carla paused, silverware in midair, and frowned at the deep brown splotch just under the ribbed neckline. "Oh geez!" she said, then frantically dipped her napkin in her water glass and dabbed at the stain, so it faded yet spread wetly across the fluffy strands of angora yarn, flattening them. "I just bought this last week too. It's a Versace."

"Too bad," said Liz. That stain might never come out. But it probably didn't matter much to Carla, who no doubt had a few dozen new sweaters nestled in the drawers of her elaborate walk-in closet. Maybe because her dress wasn't designer, Carla deemed it beneath her notice. The thought rankled Liz. She wasn't Carla's broke temp anymore with a limited wardrobe. She was an editor now and hopefully never had to make copies for the likes of Carla again, or fetch pens and paper from the supply closet, or traverse long hallways of the bank on errands that Carla was too fat and lazy to do herself. At last, one of Kent's start-up companies was making a decent profit.

"I hope I don't spill on my dress," said Liz, sitting forward a little to place the dress closer in Carla's line of vision. But Carla was intent on scrubbing her widening stain, looking down at an angle that made the pouch under her chin balloon cartoonishly. Her forehead was dotted with dung-colored age spots. Even her hands were spotted. She hadn't been aging well at all. "Hopefully it will come out at the cleaners," Liz noted, wondering if Carla maybe had a touch of dementia.

"Yah," said Carla, still dabbing at the stain. "I'm taking a load of clothes to the cleaners Friday." The server appeared with their wine and a bright smile.

"Lovely!" said Liz. She drained her glass then grabbed the fresh one. The heat of the wine was pressing on her chest and head, activating her resentment at both Carla and herself. Why couldn't she just say no to Carla, even after all this time? Not only was Carla rude and insensitive as a supervisor and a drinking buddy, but as rich as she was, she had the annoying habits of "forgetting" to bring cash for tips and then "forgetting" she borrowed money. Liz recalled her tab was up to about $50.

Carla grasped the stem of her wine glass with her oddly spotted fingers. "So, do you miss our happy hours?" she asked with a sly smile. "We were quite the team, huh?" Carla had a smear of egg on her upper lip that she rescued with her tongue. Liz cringed.

After long days of supervising Liz's clerical tasks for Carla's demanding VP boss, Carla had introduced her to the downtown happy hour scene, where she shocked Liz with her transformation from chatting matron to bold flirt after a few drinks, initiating dancing, chugging contests, singalongs and other shenanigans. Once she even flung off her shirt after starting a strip poker game when she saw some guy had a deck of cards, then disappeared with him without so much as a word. Broke, lonely and separated from Kent at the time, Liz had nothing better to do but lift a glass and join in the fun. Since then Liz had reconciled with Kent and she was now happily married. Thank goodness.

"That was so long ago. I hardly remember," Liz said, disgusted by the idea of working as a happy hour team with Carla, although Carla's antics and her own quiet good looks did attract a lot of male attention back then. "We're knee-deep in men," Liz had once said laughingly to

Carla, trying unsuccessfully to match tequila shots with her.

"Oh, come on," said Carla. "How about that kid you ripped off? Don't tell me you don't remember that."

"What are you talking about, Carla? What kid? What the heck?" demanded Liz.

"Shusshhh!" Carla hissed, her eyes bulging toward a nearby table, where a couple of men in suits were laughing over beers and burgers. "There's businesspeople here."

Liz drained her glass then slammed it down on the table, outrage welling up in her. What was Carla trying to pull? And since when was Carla a beacon of morality? Carla was the one who'd joyfully cheated on her husband throughout their marriage as he paid the bills then politely died, leaving her a small fortune from his trucking business.

This was it. Definitely her last lunch with Carla. Who was Carla anyway? Some sort of hillbilly from up north. She'd made vague references to trailer parks and family members in prison. How dare Carla shush her!

"Get lost, Carla," Liz said, finally.

"We're done here," Carla pronounced, then waved her hand at the server, who nodded from the other end of the diner.

"Oh really?" Liz fumed. She didn't think she could sit here much longer without throwing something at Carla. Maybe her dirty fork, or even her leftover-encrusted plate.

Carla was running her tongue along her upper lip, eyes locked insolently with Liz's. The server hurried over, her smile tense. "Here you go, ladies," she said, setting the bill in the middle of the table. Liz slammed down a twenty and a ten without looking at the bill.

"Keep the change," Liz said, sliding into her coat as

Carla squinted at the bill, probably trying to figure if Liz had left enough change to cover the tip.

Liz huddled in her VW Beetle, waiting for the inadequate heater to kick in. It was cold for early November and now it was snowing. Carla was taking her sweet time, as usual. Or maybe she'd called an Uber and left through another door, leaving her to endlessly wait. Liz was tempted to drive away without her, but as angry as she was, she couldn't just leave Carla here. She didn't leave people places.

"At last," Liz muttered. Carla was waddling toward the car in her flashy silver leather jacket, her bleached hair whipping around her big, self-absorbed face in the wind. As usual, Carla seemed concerned only about herself and her immediate needs, like shoving her squat torso into the passenger seat while making loud huffing and puffing noises. As soon as Carla fastened the seat belt over her wide self, Liz pulled out of the parking lot and into the street as windshield wipers furiously battled the pelting snowflakes. Carla's knee was knocking against hers in the compact front seat. Liz tried to pull away, cursing the tiny, cold car.

"I wouldn't rip off any kid," Liz claimed into the snowy silence as she aimed the car through the upcoming green light. "I don't steal from people."

"Oh yeah?" asked Carla. "What about that bracelet you're wearing then?"

"Bracelet?" asked Liz. She lifted her arm to see her gold bracelet slide from her wrist and disappear under her coat sleeve. She'd almost forgotten she was wearing it: the bracelet she'd taken from Mrs. Bergman's jewelry box as a teen. Mrs. Bergman had so many gold bangles. And she was just a poor babysitter. But how on earth...?

"Look out!" screamed Carla, over the sudden blare of a truck horn.

Liz looked up just in time to see the hulking grille of the oncoming truck slam into the side of the VW with a sickeningly loud crash. The last thing she knew was an enormous, crushing pain.

***

LIZ WONDERED why she could never say no to Carla. Here she was again, wearing her nice green dress and accessorized to the nines, as if she and Carla were traditional ladies who lunched and had vacation homes and charities to discuss. Carla didn't seem to notice her dress, or her, really. In fact, Carla looked so far around the bend today, expecting anything from her was probably a lost cause. Carla was really letting herself go. Her nice white sweater was filthy. Didn't she stain it during their last lunch? She hadn't bothered to get it cleaned. The dark bean stain was still emblazoned across the front and the cuff was still brown, like she'd been playing in a mud puddle. Here Carla was, free of her husband at last after years of cheating, and she wasn't exactly dateable. Some of the liver spots dotting her face and hands were raised, like warts. And her eyes, under her jutting forehead, were popping so far out of their sockets Liz thought she might have a touch of Grave's disease, the thyroid condition that caused these symptoms in Liz's cousin.

Not to mention Carla's odd behaviour. She'd barely touched her James Dean. She just sat watching the swarm of fruit flies circling the sandwich. This diner was really going downhill, too. Fruit flies? Liz was mad at herself for being here, as if she were still Carla's temp, at her beck and call. She had an urge to make this a liquid lunch, but she needed to work on her book reviews this afternoon and didn't want to be tipsy. She'd put off her book reviews for so long, she couldn't remember what the books were. She shoved her huevos rancheros around on her plate and took a small bite.

Liz was about to break the uncomfortable silence with an inquiry about Carla's long-ailing shoulder, when she saw that Carla was flicking her tongue at the fruit flies, like she wanted to catch them, amphibian-style.

"Carla!" Liz squealed. "What are you doing?"

Carla snapped her tongue back in her mouth and gave Liz an embarrassed look. "Oh," she said, as if remembering where she was. "Sorry. I got a frozen shoulder, you know. My doctor says to me, he says the range of motion is down thirty percent from normal."

"Oh," Liz said, wondering if Carla had done some tippling before lunch. Or maybe she had dementia.

"How are you ladies doing?" asked their usual server, who looked really tired and more silly than usual in her puffy 1950s poodle skirt and bobby socks. Her ear lobes were drooping under the weight of multiple earrings. Her skull and tiger tattoos stared balefully from the dry pallor of her arms. She smiled determinedly at them. "Can I get you ladies another glass of wine?"

"Sure," said Liz.

"I'm fine," Carla replied. Strangely, Carla's glass was still full of Chardonnay.

Carla had stopped lunching altogether, and was just sitting there, shoulders hunched, staring at her. Fortunately, the server was back in a flash with the wine, setting Liz's glass before her. Liz gulped her Merlot. She'd just finish this glass and leave, but she wasn't looking forward to Carla getting into her car or driving out there in the dangerous snowy conditions, judging by what was coming down outside the window.

"Remember the happy hour when were knee-deep in men, all the way to the door, and that guy was giving us massages?" Liz asked, trying to sound cheerful. Maybe the memory of men would stop Carla staring at her as if she were one of the fruit flies still flitting around her James Dean.

Liz was relieved to see Carla's wide smile, but where were her teeth? "Oh yah! And how about that kid we fooled around with there, the one you ripped off?"

The kid again. Carla emphasized her accusal by pointing at her; one of her ruder gestures, Liz thought, then saw Carla's fingers were connected by actual webbing.

"What the heck, Carla?" Liz squealed. She wondered if she was hallucinating. Maybe they drugged her. The server must have put something in her wine, and maybe her food.

Carla's spotted face darkened with disapproval. "Shusssshhhh!" she sputtered. "There's professionals here!" Carla's eyes, rotating on their extended sockets, shot a protective look at the two men at the next table. To Liz's horror, they were covered in scales and squirming around in their suits.

Liz put her head in her hands. She had to be hallucinating. Even so, she was enraged that Carla had the gall to shush her. This wasn't the first time either. Could Carla have slipped some LSD in her wine?

She looked up at Carla, resisting the urge to toss her wine in her face.

"What kid?" she asked between clenched teeth.

"You know," said Carla. "The kid we did tequila shots with at Dan Sweeney's. Kissy kissy, remember?" She puckered the spotted ridge of her mouth that used to be her lips.

Liz remembered reluctantly. Those drunken days were such a blur. There was a young IT guy, fresh out of college, with apple cheeks and puppy-bright laughing eyes, who said something about them being "party girls." Liz had found that hilariously flattering. Doing tequila shots with this kid in his crisp button-down shirt, young enough to be her son and calling her a girl, seemed like a hysterical prank. She remembered Carla's hand on his arm. "Liz's my temp. She works under me," she'd told him with a lewd wink. This had to be the kid.

"I didn't rip him off," Liz insisted. "What are you talking about?"

"Oh come on," urged Carla, the pouch under her chin quivering. "Don't you remember the taxi ride home? Kissy kissy, huh?"

Kissy, kissy. The hazy, drunken memory was surfacing like a migraine. She'd heard that before, in the cab on the way home from the bar. The kid was lolling between them, his arms around them as the cab came to a stop in some quiet area. He giggled and called them party girls under their kisses. "Kissy, kissy," Carla cooed. Carla's face, her eyes raccoonish with smeared makeup, had loomed close to hers, over his, over hers?

"Are these Dockers?" she remembered asking him, to great hilarity. Then his wallet was in her hand. She'd paid the fare out of it. Had he given her permission? She couldn't remember.

"You ripped him off," accused Carla.

"I gave him his wallet back!" she insisted. That she remembered.

"After bagging a few bills for yourself," Carla said. "For services rendered. And you didn't even share it with me." Her toad mouth drooped suggestively.

"Once a thief, always a thief. I knew you swiped that bracelet from Mrs. Bergman, for example."

Liz looked down at her gold bangle encircling the green cuff of her dress. Carla had accused her of this before, she remembered, in the snow. Just before the big thing slammed into them... the huge, horrible truck. She shuddered recalling the excruciating pain, but it had lasted barely a second and seemed to have happened in another world. Or in a dream. Or was she dreaming now?

"And how about that fancy Barbie doll dress you took from little Carrie Stevenson when you were five?" Carla continued, amphibian eyes with horizontal pupils focused on her like in some nature show. "And all the clothes you swiped at The Loft, when you were living in the dorms there. You were a good little shoplifter, too. Some of those sweaters were cute."

The pouch under Carla's chin puffed and quivered as she counted off more of Liz's petty thefts and indiscretions on her fingers, or maybe they were her toes now. She only had four on each hand, or foot.

"I was just a kid," Liz protested, as if that were more important than Carla turning into an omniscient toad. What really worried her was Carla dredging up any more men who partied with them. What if Kent found out?

"You were no kid when you plagiarized that ad copy for the Blue Door account," Carla sneered with her ridge of a mouth. "You stole that ad copy from the Krenzen Agency so you'd get the account but that didn't work out so good for you, did it? Once a thief, always a thief." Carla gave a sad shake of her knobby head.

The Blue Door account. Liz's Waterloo. All she'd done was cut and paste some copy from another website to meet a deadline, and she'd even changed the key words. But it was enough to get her fired from Crandall Mitchum, leading to a desultory stint of clerical temp work and eventually to her fateful assignment at the bank, where Carla was waiting.

"Who are you?" Liz asked, careful not to swear again. One of the guys at the next table had unhinged his jaw to fit a whole ham into his gaping mouth.

Carla's neck pouch swelled to the size of a beach ball, ripping open her white sweater and even her lacy bra underneath. Her turquoise necklace popped off and flew to the floor. A victorious croak burst from her maw. Carla was now a human-sized toad, only recognizable by the shredded white angora yarn clinging to her arms, or technically her legs.

"This has to be hell," Liz said, recoiling from Carla's bumpy swollen pouch. The two snake guys next to them were slithering out of their suits. More creatures, human-sized lizards and amphibians were leaping on tables and crawling around after terrified lunchers.

"Well, it ain't heaven, kiddo," croaked Carla, with a loud, rasping laugh that sounded like she was choking on sand. "It was gonna happen for us sooner or later."

"But I hardly did enough to warrant eternal damnation," Liz heard herself whine.

"That's just it. You didn't do enough. It's the way you let things happen, you know. You coulda put up more of a fight. But you let yourself slide into my swamp, kiddo. You were such an obedient little thing at the bank, too. I bet you'd still let me hop into your car after lunch today, you're so wishy-washy."

Liz chafed at the critique but she knew it was true. All this time Liz thought Carla was ignoring her, when in fact she knew so much about her she was bored by it all. She looked hopelessly out the window. Would it always be snowing? Her last memory of being outdoors would be the huge truck grille smashing her and Carla into their entwined doom. "I'm not your temp anymore," she protested.

"You got that right. You're on permanent now, kiddo. You knew deep down you'd find me shopping at the Galleria last week. It was your destiny. Our destiny." Like some rainforest toad but for the torn bra flapping under her front leg, Carla hopped onto the table.

Liz screamed and almost toppled over in her chair, but Carla was only snapping at a moth. When Liz moved her wine glass safely out of the way of Carla's big warty foot, she screamed again at what she saw on her own hand. Scales! They were a mottled green colour, ending in black claws. This had to be a dream or a hallucination. She reached in her purse for her compact mirror but decided she didn't want to see whatever reptilian face she had.

"Hey fellas, how's it goin'" Carla croaked at the two snake guys, her toad mouth twisting flirtatiously.

The server was back, her smile exhausted and her hair streaked with gray. "Can I get you another glass?" she asked Liz with a pitying look.

"Sure," said Liz. If this was really hell, there wouldn't be wine. "Actually, could you please bring over a few bottles?"

The Idea Trust

John Leahy

It was after nine when Sabine Greer summoned them to the top floor. That mattered— 9:03 p.m., to be exact. Too late for dinner, too early for midnight strategy. It was the hour of extraction, when the ambitious were made to prove their worth, and the loyal were tested for blood content. The email arrived with a subject line like a knife:

"Executive Briefing. Top Deck. Now."

No signature. Sabine didn't need one.

The elevator hummed like something old and thoughtful. Zeke Manzinger stood alone in it, glancing at his reflection in the brushed steel panelling which looked flatter than he felt. He hadn't shaved. The shirt he'd thrown on was rumpled, vaguely blue. His eyes were still vibrating from the last ten hours of debug, but this wasn't something you begged off from. Sabine called, you went. Even if it was to your own funeral.

The top floor opened like a stage: matte-black floors, seamless glass walls, no art, no signage. Just the lights of the sleeping city blinking below like idiot stars.

Zelda Grosvenor and her assistant Voight were already in the boardroom when Zeke walked in. She wore her usual legal armour: steel-coloured blouse, matte lipstick, eyes that didn't blink without consulting a strategy. Voight stood behind her like a lacquered mannequin, tablet in hand.

Sabine arrived last. She entered without sound, as if gravity didn't fully apply to her. Black silk blouse, tailored charcoal pants, nothing decorative—unless you counted the faint platinum threadwork at her cuffs. Her eyes scanned them in one quiet sweep and dismissed their humanity without cruelty, just efficiency.

"Let's begin," she said, sitting.

Zeke dropped into the seat at her left. His legs didn't want to stop twitching. He flattened his glass pad on the table, fingers jittery. "You want to see the monster."

"I said that?" Sabine asked, one eyebrow twitching upward.

"You said 'show us the monster'." Zeke didn't look at her. He was calling up the projection.

"I was being generous," she said. "Most monsters have more charm."

The table flickered. A cloud of neural mapping bloomed above it—soft light, rotating vectors, pulsing nodes. At first it looked like a weather system. Then it pulsed and twisted and began to hum faintly, like a sleeping brain dreaming too fast.

"Start explaining," Zelda said. Her voice was always dry, but now it had a crispness like cold air through blinds.

Zeke tapped. New overlays flickered into place—gold bursts, blue flicks, spirals of data. "What you're seeing," Zeke began, "are real-time delta-spike events. We're mapping live brain activity from CogiNet-implanted users.

These..." He pointed at the gold bursts "... are moments of high-coherence novelty. Not recall, not repetition. This is ideation. Original thought. Lightning hitting sand."

"You're capturing it?" Zelda asked. Her voice was flat, but her fingers flexed just slightly.

"No," Zeke said. "We're sieving it. The system watches for spikes that pass a certain originality threshold. When they do, it models them—no storage, no raw data retention. Just vectors. Then the engine scores them."

"And when something scores high?"

"We recreate it. Model to form. Reverse the pattern into an exportable construct. From there, it enters development. Under black NDA silos."

Zelda stared at him. "You're stealing thoughts."

"No," Zeke said. "We're interpreting fireworks. Not stealing—translating. It's ambient cognition. Passive signal. Think of it like... weather telemetry for ideas."

Sabine was sipping black coffee in a cup as minimalist as her personality. "Weather?" she murmured.

"Okay," Zeke said. "Oil. From shale."

"That's not a legal analogy," Zelda snapped.

Sabine didn't even smile. "It's a metaphor. Get me indicted for the right reasons, not for bad poetry."

Zelda's sigh was silent. Voight adjusted nothing.

"I need clarity," Sabine said, setting her cup down with surgical precision. "Are we exposed?"

Zelda looked at Voight, who answered in a tone so flat it might have been code.

"The latest CogiNet update includes bundled Cognitive Enhancement Services. Buried in the health optimization agreement."

"Explicit consent?" Zelda asked.

"No," Voight said. "Consent by use. Standard passive telemetry clause."

"Nobody reads those."

"Correct."

Sabine nodded once. "So they opted in. Even if they didn't know they were opting in."

"That won't hold up in court if a plaintiff shows IP theft," Zelda warned. "If we pull something too close to their lived memory…"

"We don't store memory," Zeke said.

"Doesn't matter," Zelda said. "If they feel it was stolen —if it *feels* like theirs, and the product looks close—they'll come. Class action. Ethics board. FTC if we're lucky. DOJ if we're not."

"We can gate it," Zeke said. "We can mask outputs."

"You can't unbirth an idea," Zelda snapped. "Once it's out, it *looks* like theft. Truth won't matter."

"Then we lie better," Sabine said. Calmly. Coldly.

The boardroom fell into that kind of hush you get before a scalpel touches skin. The projection rotated slowly, casting stray reflections on the glass walls. Somewhere far below, sirens whispered through the city. No one acknowledged them. Zelda shifted in her seat. The motion was minor, but it felt like a signal flare.

"Let's be clear," she said, looking directly at Sabine. "If someone matches a monetized concept to their own spike pattern—even once—it opens the door. Doesn't matter how you filter it or bury the pipeline. We're in the territory of involuntary IP generation. The implications…"

"Are theoretical," Sabine interrupted. "So far, nothing's leaked."

"So far," Zelda echoed, tight-lipped.

Sabine turned to Zeke. "Your neural sieve. Could it ever accidentally reassemble too much?"

Zeke hesitated. That pause cost him.

"Yes or no," Sabine said.

"It depends," he said, finally. "We have suppression logic in place. If the system senses excessive coherence with prior memory clusters, it drops the pattern. But novelty rides the edge. If someone dreams something genuinely new... and remembers it afterward..."

"They might recognize it," Zelda said, tone clipped. "That's the exposure point."

Sabine folded her hands on the table. "Then we close the loop. Attribution. Voight?"

The assistant spoke without raising his head. "We seed system-originated ideation into a shell entity. Assign joint authorship to the platform. Attribution defaults to the trust."

"The Idea Trust," Sabine said, smiling now. "So lovely and vague."

Zelda squinted. "You're laundering thought."

"We're clarifying origin," Voight corrected. Still hadn't blinked.

"Same thing," Zeke murmured.

"No," Sabine said. "One is illegal. The other is innovation."

She stood, slowly. Walked to the glass wall. Fog was climbing the skyline now, flowing between buildings like something patient and uninvited.

"Here's what we know," she said, facing the window. "Human cognition is inefficient. Uneven. Glorious, yes, but wasteful. How many ideas are born at 2 a.m. and never leave the pillow? How much beauty rots in silence?"

Silence.

"We harvest genius," she said softly. "That's our work. Not extraction. Not theft. Elevation."

Behind her, Zelda closed her eyes for a moment. "I'm a lawyer," she said. "Not a philosopher. The risk is definable."

Sabine turned back. "So, define it."

Zelda inhaled through her nose. "Worst case? Congressional hearings. Whistleblowers. Tech press crucifixion. If even one user's spike matches a product launch… perfectly…we lose control of the narrative."

Sabine tilted her head. "Then don't let it match perfectly."

Zeke raised both eyebrows. "You want us to *weaken* the reconstructions?"

"I want you to *distill* them," Sabine said. "Derivative enough to avoid recognition. Powerful enough to market."

"That's threading a needle blindfolded," Zeke muttered.

"But possible," Sabine said. "And you'll find a way."

Zelda gave a small, bitter laugh. "Ethics board will demand access. Eventually."

"Then we give them a sandbox," Sabine said. "Low-tier data. Volunteer spikes. Let them prod the corpse while the real body keeps breathing elsewhere."

"Obfuscation," Zelda said.

Sabine met her gaze. "Containment."

Voight's tablet chirped once. He acknowledged it with a blink. "Soft probe from internal compliance," he said. "Likely automated. Minor anomaly flag."

Sabine smiled thinly. "They're early."

Zelda leaned forward. "We'll need obfuscation trees.

Legal filters. A triple-blind pipeline from spike to prototype."

"Already designed," Voight said. "Requires board sign-off. But we've baked in plausible disassociation."

Sabine was silent for a moment. Then she moved back to her seat, slow and deliberate. Lowered herself into it like a monarch reclaiming the throne. "I want this clean," she said. "I want the system surgically precise. I want a wall between us and the fire."

"And if someone gets burned anyway?" Zelda asked.

Sabine shrugged. "Then we offer them a job. Or a settlement. Whichever's cheaper."

Zeke rubbed his temples. "You don't understand the implications. If we ever let something *too big* through… something *real*…"

Sabine turned her eyes on him, and for a moment, the room felt colder. "What do you mean, too real?"

"I mean… something disruptive. Groundbreaking. An idea so pure it could pivot industries. Rewrite markets. If we let something like *that* go public…"

"Then we don't," Sabine said. "We sit on it."

Zelda stared. "You'd bury a breakthrough?"

Sabine's voice dropped to a whisper, sharp as a pin. "Power is the *timing* of truth."

Zeke's gaze didn't waver. "Let me ask something fundamental. Who owns an idea that never fully belonged to any one person? This system is pulling fragments from thousands of brains. Threads woven together, emerging into something 'new'."

Sabine smiled faintly, but it was tight. "Ownership is a social contract, not a natural law. We're rewriting the terms."

Zelda interjected, voice measured but firm. "Legally, IP law requires a human author. AI co-authorship is still uncharted territory, but courts lean toward *human* creativity."

"Which is why we insert the Idea Trust as a legal fiction," Voight said, finally breaking his robotic stillness. "It's a vessel—an entity without corporeal form—owning the IP. The trust licenses the rights out to subsidiaries and R&D teams. It's a buffer."

Zelda folded her hands again, steepling her fingers. "But what if a user insists an idea came directly from their mind? They can prove the spike signature matches the final product."

Sabine's eyes gleamed in the dim light. "Then they get bought out. A non-disclosure agreement, severance, maybe even a consulting role."

Zeke scoffed. "You're buying silence. What about those who refuse? Or those who demand royalties?"

"Rare," Sabine said, shrugging elegantly. "And expensive. The risk pool is smaller than you think. Our user base is vast. We can absorb losses."

Zelda tapped a fingernail on the glass surface. "Absorb, yes, but only for so long. Public sentiment can flip overnight. You saw what happened with the NeurAlpha leaks last year."

Sabine nodded slowly. "That was an amateur hour compared to us. We're different. This is precision engineering—biometric telemetry refined to a scalpel's edge."

Voight's voice came out quiet but insistent. "We can anonymize data streams more aggressively. We already patch spikes with synthetic noise patterns to prevent forensic tracing."

Zelda gave a skeptical glance. "Synthetic noise—sounds like obfuscation on steroids. Regulators will smell that eventually."

Sabine leaned forward, fingers interlaced. "Regulators are always late. That's a fact. We move fast. Outpace their grasp."

Zeke shook his head. "We're building a house on quicksand. Sooner or later, it'll collapse."

"Or sink to reveal new foundations," Sabine countered. "We're not just creating ideas. We're creating a new economy of thought."

Zelda exhaled. "An economy where thoughts are harvested, owned, and traded like commodities."

"Exactly." Sabine's smile returned. "And we're the bankers."

Silence settled.

Zeke finally broke it. "What about the user experience? If someone feels violated…"

"Compensation," Sabine said smoothly. "And a choice. They can opt out of the Cognitive Enhancement Services at any time."

Zelda's eyebrows lifted. "Opt-out. Meaning?"

"You lose access to the network's advanced features," Voight said. "Suboptimal health metrics. Reduced cognitive throughput."

"Economic incentives," Sabine added. "Opting out carries penalties. But technically, it's voluntary."

Zelda shook her head, frustration seeping in. "Voluntary under duress. Classic."

Sabine laughed softly. "You sound like a cynic, Zelda. That's not bad. Keep your cynicism sharp. It keeps us honest."

Zelda's eyes narrowed. "Or it keeps us from breaking the law."

Sabine's gaze flicked to the door. "That's what you're here for. To keep us legal."

Zeke looked at Zelda, then back to Sabine. "And if you ask me? We're dancing on a razor's edge. One misstep, and the whole system falls apart."

Sabine rose again. "Then we practise balance. Like tightrope walkers, only with better nets."

Voight's tablet chimed again. "Compliance has escalated to phase two. Preparing preliminary audit report."

Sabine nodded. "Good. Let them come. We'll meet them in the sandbox."

Zelda exhaled sharply. "Sandbox or not, this is the future of cognition. And it's terrifying."

Sabine smiled, almost affectionately. "Good. Fear breeds respect. Respect breeds caution. And caution breeds longevity."

The room grew colder, shadows lengthening as fog gathered outside. The city below was a blur of lights and whispers—an unseen audience to the birth of a new era. Sabine settled back into her chair, the black silk of her blouse rippling like dark water. "Let's circle back. Consent. The heart of this beast."

Zelda exhaled slowly, gaze fixed on the glass table's polished surface. "You say users consent through the CogiNet firmware update. But consent isn't just a checkbox on a license agreement."

Voight's expression remained unreadable, but his voice was calm, rehearsed. "The Cognitive Enhancement Services are embedded within the health optimization license. It's explicit, if dense."

Zelda laughed—sharp, brittle. "Dense. The perfect euphemism for unreadable legalese. We're not talking about consenting to a newsletter. This is your *brain*. Your *thoughts*."

Sabine's lips curved. "Yes. And yet, no one reads terms and conditions. No one ever has. The market dictates behaviour. If people want the latest cognitive edge, they swallow the pill whole, no questions asked."

Zeke shook his head. "That's complacency, not consent. And dangerous complacency at that."

Zelda leaned forward, hands animated. "Imagine a user, somewhere, who discovers their own neural spike was harvested and monetized without clear knowledge. They'd feel violated. Maybe exploited."

Sabine tilted her head, considering. "Then they sue. And we settle. Quietly. Expensively. But rarely publicly. Our settlements are sealed. We never admit wrongdoing."

Zeke's eyes flashed. "And if one of those cases goes public? The backlash would be catastrophic."

"Not if we're proactive," Sabine said smoothly. "Which is why we're building layers of legal and technical defences. The Idea Trust. The synthetic noise. The opt-out penalties. It's a fortress."

Zelda tapped her nails. "But walls can be breached."

"We make sure the moat is full," Sabine countered. "The moat filled with disincentives, legal thorns, public relations shields."

Voight finally broke his silence, voice quiet but firm. "We're also rolling out an educational campaign. Targeted ads, tutorials, even VR experiences to help users understand what they're signing up for. Make consent feel less like an ambush."

Zelda gave a skeptical glance. "Good luck making that feel genuine."

Sabine's eyes glittered. "The illusion of choice is sometimes enough."

Zeke sighed. "At what cost? We're eroding the very idea of intellectual ownership."

Zelda nodded. "And personal sovereignty."

Sabine's voice dropped, conspiratorial. "Sovereignty is a relic in the age of networks. We're all nodes in a larger system now. Resistance is quaint."

Zelda's jaw tightened. "Quaint? It's human dignity."

Sabine shrugged. "Call it what you will. I call it evolution."

Zeke stared at her, disbelieving. "Evolution that strips us of our minds' sanctity? That's not evolution. It's extinction."

Sabine's smile was thin but unwavering. "Then it's a good thing *we're* steering the ship, not you."

Zelda folded her arms. "Sabine, I'm here to protect this company from legal ruin. But sometimes, I wonder if I'm protecting something worse."

The room hung heavy with unsaid truths.

Sabine's voice softened, almost gentle. "You're protecting survival. Innovation isn't pretty. It's a war zone."

Zeke looked away, rubbing his temples. "I don't know if I can keep doing this."

Sabine's eyes locked on his. "Then maybe you shouldn't."

Zelda's voice was quieter now, but no less firm. "We need guardrails. Not just for the company, but for people."

Sabine nodded slowly. "Guardrails. Fine. But they'll be made of steel. Not velvet."

Voight's tablet chimed again, breaking the tension. "Compliance audit is ready for review."

Sabine rose. "Show me."

Zeke swiped the glass tablet, and the room dimmed as the projection lit up again. This time it was a sprawling compliance matrix, a labyrinthine network of protocols, risk assessments, and regulatory checkpoints.

Sabine's eyes flicked over the data with a practised eye. "Looks thorough."

Zelda's tone was tight. "The auditors dug deep. They've identified potential weak points, especially around minors and medical data interfaces."

"The system's sandbox trial helped" Voight added. "Volunteer data showed no breaches. But it's a controlled environment."

"Controlled means sanitized," Zeke said. "Real-world users aren't sanitized."

Sabine tapped her fingers, a slow rhythm. "We're launching a layered rollout. Sandbox first. Then scaled opt-in. Full system locked behind a multi-tiered security protocol. We buy time."

Zelda shook her head. "Time isn't on our side. Laws will catch up."

Sabine smiled. "They always do. But they're slow. Clumsy. The market moves faster."

Zeke grimaced. "Faster doesn't mean better."

Sabine turned to him. "Better is subjective. Right now, it's survival and profit."

Zelda frowned. "And what about trust? Public trust?"

Sabine's voice dropped, almost cold. "Public trust is a fragile commodity. We manage it with controlled transparency and strategic opacity."

Voight chimed in, "The PR team is ready with narratives. 'Empowering the Mind', 'Unlocking Human Potential', and the like."

Zelda snorted. "Spin. Always spin."

Sabine shrugged. "Spin sells. Ethics, unfortunately, don't pay the bills."

Zeke stood suddenly, the tension radiating off him. "I didn't sign up for a moral black hole."

Sabine's gaze sharpened. "Nobody ever does."

Zelda exhaled, her eyes meeting Zeke's. "We're at a crossroads. One path leads to groundbreaking innovation, the other to ethical quagmire."

Sabine folded her hands on the table. "And the third?"

Zelda blinked. "What third?"

Sabine's smile was slow, almost predatory. "The third path is what we create ourselves. We don't wait for law or morality to catch up. We *lead*. We redefine the game."

Voight nodded. "Pioneer or pariah. Choice is ours."

Zeke shook his head, voice low. "Or maybe it's no choice at all. Maybe we're just passengers on this runaway train."

Zelda's voice softened. "Sabine, is this a future we want?"

Sabine's eyes gleamed with cold fire. "It's the future we'll have. Because we're the ones building it."

A heavy silence settled. Outside, the fog thickened, swallowing the city lights. Sabine rose, gathering her tablets. "Meeting adjourned. Get me the rollout timeline and contingency protocols on my desk by tomorrow. And Zeke…"

He looked up sharply.

"Keep the failsafe ready. No surprises."

He nodded slowly, the weight of the night settling on his shoulders.

Zelda stood as well, voice resolute. "I'll draft a memo for the ethics board. They'll want answers."

Sabine's parting glance was sharp. "Answers can wait."

The doors hissed closed behind them as they left one by one, leaving the boardroom empty but charged. Like the calm before a storm.

The End

Did you enjoy *Unseen Agreements*?
Please consider leaving a review on Goodreads, Bookbub, or your favorite retailer.

Join our newsletter for new releases, sales and ucoming events at www.beachesandtrailspublishing.com

Contributors

Lena Samson, Editor 🍁

Lena Samson is an editor and writer living near Ottawa. She serves on the Board of Directors of Ottawa Independent Writers (OIW) and as Editor in Chief of their annual anthology. Lena has edited fiction, non-fiction, alternative history, memoir and children's books (so far), as well as stories in all genres. Retired from the federal public service, Lena enjoys grandmothering, editing, writing and trying to please her fussy pet rabbit.

Abby Andresen

Since publishing her darkly comic novel *An Inappropriate Crush* in 2017, Abby Andresen has found a niche writing psychological horror. Her eerie stories, inspired by Shirley Jackson, Joyce Carol Oates and other women writers of dark fiction, have appeared in several horror anthologies. Prior to finding her voice in fiction, Abby worked as a standup comedian, freelance writer, and vintage clothing dealer. She lives in Minneapolis with her spirit cat and she's thrilled to have a story in *Unseen Agreements*.

Bella Chacha

Bella Chacha is a Nigerian writer whose work explores memory, myth, and resilience. Her stories and essays have appeared in *Brittle Paper*, *IHRAM Publishes*, *Channel*, *Cosmic Daffodil*, and *Heartlines Spec*, with forthcoming work in *Wrath Bona Book*. A finalist for the 2025 Defenestrationism.net Short Story Contest, she continues to craft narratives that blend the speculative with the deeply personal.

Alison Colwell [*]

Alison Colwell is a writer, mother, domestic violence survivor and community organizer. She writes both fiction and creative nonfiction, and her work has been published in several literary journals including *The Humber Literary Review, Hippocampus Magazine, Dorothy Parker's Ashes, The Orange & Bee Magazine,* and *Crow & Cross Keys Magazine.* She lives on Galiano Island, Canada.

Andrew Dunlop [*]

Andrew Dunlop is a horror, science fiction, and fantasy author and poet living and working in Ontario, Canada. When not writing, Andrew is a tabletop gamer and enjoys painting landscapes and recreational running. Andrew lives with a loving partner and an extremely opinionated parrot.

RP Ferguson

RP Ferguson is an Arizona-based author who loves crafting fantastical stories. His background in education and behavioural health has inspired him to create characters that are complex and relatable. Regardless of genre, RP believes characters are the heartbeat of every story. In addition to writing fiction and poetry, RP has also written a script for a video game that is in active development

Daniel Fox [*]

Daniel Fox is a writer of horror, thrillers, fantasy, and children's books. He also created an online choose-your-own-adventure horror video game called *Ocean of Death*. Wow, he should really focus.

Elizabeth Hosang

Elizabeth is an author of short stories in the genres of mystery, science fiction and fantasy, one of which was a finalist for the 2017 Crime Writers of Canada Award of Excellence. Her work has appeared in over twenty anthologies, and in 2024 she collected some of her early works in a self-published collection.

John Leahy

John Leahy has had three novels published: *Harvest*, *CROGIAN*, and *Unity*. His short story "Singers" was included in Flame Tree Publishing's 2017 *Pirates and Ghosts* anthology, alongside tales by literary greats such as Homer, Rudyard Kipling, Arthur Conan Doyle, H.P. Lovecraft, and H.G. Wells. He lives in Killarney, Ireland.

Marie-Hélène Lebeault 🍁

Marie-Hélène Lebeault is a Canadian speculative fiction author whose creations blend magic, mystery, and emotional depth. Author of 30+ titles, including *The Evers Series, Blood Magick Trilogy, Defenders of the Realm, Legends Reborn, North Pole University* and the *Fairy Grandmother* picture book series, her work spans young adult, adult fantasy and sci-fi.

Kathryn Riley

Kathryn Riley has taught linguistics and writing at several universities and has published research in both subject areas. She currently lives near Atlanta, Georgia and is at work on a novel and a story collection.

Lynne Sargent 🍁

Lynne Sargent is a queer writer, aerialist, and holds a Ph.D. in Applied Philosophy. They are the poetry editor at *Utopia Science Fiction* magazine. Their work has been nominated for Rhysling, Elgin, and Aurora Awards, and has appeared in venues such as *Augur Magazine*, *Strange Horizons*, and *Analog*.

Jesse Scoble 🍁

Jesse Scoble is co-writer of *Dead Money*, a Western horror comic. He is an award-winning video game and tabletop role-playing game writer, and has worked on best-selling table-top role-playing games. A senior narrative designer for Beamdog, Jesse lives in Montreal. He is publishing his first novel, *Just a Game*, in 2026.

About the Publisher

Beaches and Trails Publishing is an independent Canadian press based in Quebec, dedicated to uplifting stories that comfort, inspire, and empower. We believe in the power of inclusive, positive, and accessible fiction.

Our catalogue highlights a diversity of Canadian voices—especially emerging authors and writers from underrepresented communities

At Beaches and Trails, every book is an invitation to feel good—and to feel seen.

www.beachesandtrailspublishing.com

instagram.com/beachesandtrailspublishing
facebook.com/beachesandtrailspublishing
amazon.com/author/beachesandtrailspublishing
linkedin.com/company/beaches-and-trails-publishing
pinterest.com/beachesandtrailspublishing
x.com/BAT_publishing

www.ingramcontent.com/pod-product-compliance
Lightning Source LLC
Chambersburg PA
CBHW020324260626
47156CB00004B/1359